STOP AT NOTHING

by John Welcome

"The scenery is splendid (the Irish foxhunting countryside, the mountains of Provence, the golden beaches of the Côte d'Azur), we travel in style (private planes, Bentleys, Mark VIII Jaguars, Ferraris), and the food and drink are excellent."

—*The New Yorker*

"Excellent dry prose." —*New Statesman*

"A de luxe mixture of thriller ingredients."

—*Times Literary Supplement*

John Welcome

STOP AT NOTHING

PERENNIAL LIBRARY
Harper & Row, Publishers
New York, Cambridge, Philadelphia, San Francisco
London, Mexico City, São Paulo, Sydney

A hardcover edition of this book was published by Alfred A. Knopf, Inc. It is here reprinted by arrangement with the Sterling Lord Agency, Inc.

First PERENNIAL LIBRARY edition published 1983.

Library of Congress Cataloging in Publication Data

Welcome, John, 1914-
  Stop at nothing.

  (Perennial library ; P/665)
  Reprint. Originally published: New York : Knopf, 1960.
  I. Title.
PR6073.E373S7 1983   823'.914   83-47588
ISBN 0-06-080665-6 (pbk.)

---

83 84 85 86 87 10 9 8 7 6 5 4 3 2 1

Contents

STOP AT NOTHING

CHAPTER 1

Young Man Angry

I was forty and I felt it. It's a bad age for an active man to be and I had always thought of myself as that. It's the first year you really feel the rot setting in and the timbers beginning to creak. It's a sort of climacteric; after your fortieth birthday you suddenly realize you are mortal.

I only decided to go to Mantovelli's party because I wanted to see what he was like and I wanted to see his house. Mildred, of course, was on for it from the beginning. She set off early in the D.K.W., driving it up through the gears as she always did. Automatically my ear tuned in to the changes. I looked out the window and watched the little green car tearing down the long avenue between the elms. However well you drove, I reflected, you could never change as crisply with a stalk on the steering column as with a short, rigid lever on the floor. And just for the record, Mildred did drive well as she did most physical things well. It was a pity we were all washed up.

I towelled myself after my bath, taking my time about it and then put on a shirt and a white collar and a regimental tie. As I pulled the knot into the collar I looked at my reflection in the glass. The tie always made me laugh when I saw myself wearing it. The members of that exclusive cavalry regiment known the world over as "Hannah's Horse", from the name of a very forceful wife of a commanding officer, never did make up their minds what they had done to deserve me. "The petrol wallah" they had christened me when I had arrived in September 1939. I had not, of course, made things any easier by announcing that I had been turned down by the Tank Corps. In the end they had learned to put up with me as most people did one way or another though it was pretty obvious that Mildred had not. On the whole, however, I decided, at least when I dressed myself up, I didn't look to have worn too badly. I might feel like the end of an old song played on a worn-out instrument sadly out of tune, but I still had my hair and my teeth and had somehow avoided the galaxy of broken blood-vessels which the years had written across so many of my contemporaries' cheek-bones.

On the strength of this I helped myself to another pink gin from the tray which we always had brought up at bath-time. As I sipped it I looked out the dressing-room window across the lush fields of Kildare to the frieze of blue mountains in the distance and wondered why I had ever come to Ireland. To dodge taxation and to satisfy some whim of Mildred's about horses, I thought, and neither of these were particularly valid reasons now.

I finished the drink on the way downstairs, left the glass on the long table in the hall and went out to the Bentley.

As I drove through the narrow country roads I thought about my host. No one knew quite who or what Mr. Mantovelli was, though he had been a world figure for a long time. A multi-millionaire, everyone had heard of his fabulous yacht, his palace in Texas, his house in Million-aires' Row and, the place he was said to love best, his mysterious mansion in Provence. His commercial interests were vast—his estate in Texas was said to be a base for his activities in oil, his yacht a tie-up with Greek shipping lines. He was almost the last of the millionaires to breed racehorses and to race on the grand scale. Success here, too, had come his way. His crop of classic winners was impressive to say the least of it. I had forgotten the number of times he had won the Two Thousand Guineas, the Leger and the Oaks. But this I did know. He had never won the Derby and he had publicly announced that he would not die until he did. As he must by now be touching eighty, even though he was said to be as tough as they come, this was pushing his luck pretty hard.

At any rate he was trying. There were stud farms in France and in Meath, private trainers in England, Ireland and France, and now he had bought Clevedon Court.

The house was genuine Adam—one of the two said to exist in Ireland where Robert Adam had come over and supervised the work himself. The Dancys had owned it— "the duelling Dancys"—and in its day it had been a famous stud, for no less than three Derby winners had been foaled there. But the last of the Dancys had been a mad old man who had lived in one room in the stableyard and had allowed the great house to fall into semi-ruin. Then he had died and Mantovelli had bought the place and restored it. He was bringing it back as a stud-farm too and there were mares there already.

Even in decay the house had been beautiful; now, with life in it again, its plaster renovated, the chipped and sagging portico restored, the serene lines of its central block and its curling colonnades outlined against the setting sun, it looked breathtakingly lovely. It was said that Mantovelli had brought over his great Cézanne collection and hung it here. If he had, I badly wanted to see it; I wanted, too, to see the interior of the house. So, one way or another, I went up the steps with a keen sense of anticipation. I little knew what I was letting myself in for.

The great flagged and pillared hall was crowded and there was the devil of a din coming from the staterooms on either side. Mantovelli had evidently cast his net pretty wide. I knew a few of the people standing about but I didn't particularly want to talk to any of them. I took a glass of champagne and started to make my way through the mob in the staterooms.

Pretty soon I ran into Maurice Kenway. One is always running into Maurice; he knows everyone and bobs up everywhere. Maurice had been in Hannah's with me; he had been my only close friend in the regiment before I left it to go to more individualistic employment which both my commanding officer and myself thought better suited to my qualities and my character. Maurice had been on the odd list, too, though not so far down it nor in such big black letters as I was. Flying your own aeroplane is socially superior to driving a racing motor-car. I can't think why.

An immensely tall, arrogant-looking chap with the face of a handsome death's head was talking to Maurice. They were discussing Maurice's new aeroplane, a Piper Apache, and the fact that he was flying out very shortly to have a look at the villa he was building in the Parc de St. Tropez.

"Stuart Jason," he said in answer to my query as the chap drifted away. "Mantovelli's right-hand man and trouble shooter."

"What's he doing? Keeping an eye on the guests?"

"Shouldn't wonder if he doesn't have to. The Dunman-ways are well under way, I see."

I followed Maurice's gaze. There they were at the end of the room and, with a sinking feeling, I recognized my wife amongst them.

Fair and florid, Sir Hector Dunmanway was holding

his court. They were just about getting to the stage when champagne bored them and they called for spirits, but at the moment, for a change, their attention was occupied by something other than drinking. A woman playwright had recently joined their circle. She announced that she received her ideas from a spirit called, I think, Walker, who communicated with her without warning and struck her into trances in the most unexpected and inconvenient places. I had noticed, however, that Walker usually seemed to get to work at parties where there was a lot of drink flying about. It was evident that he was in action now.

They had laid her reverently on a sofa when I came up, and were fussing around her almost as if one of their mares had got cast in her box.

"Is there anything we ought to do?" Mildred said to me.

"Fetch a doctor and a stomach pump, I should think," I replied, for I had my own ideas about these trances.

"Oh!" Mildred snapped at me. "Is there nothing you won't sneer at? Don't you realize that she is in touch with the spirit world?"

"Ask her what will win at Leopardstown tomorrow," I said. "It might help you with your bookie."

I heard a chuckle behind me and turned.

An old, old man, a man who had obviously been growing down into himself with age for some years, was standing at my shoulder. He was dressed in a straight-cut suit with no turn-ups on the trousers and a high, stiff, Edwardian collar was round his neck. His face was seamed and wrinkled and scarred with lines of age; he had very light blue eyes as pale and as hard as polished steel. He was leaning on a gold-headed stick and one hand held a tiny teacup.

I knew instantly who it was. M. Mantovelli the millionaire and I had met.

He raised the teacup to his lips with a gesture which I was later to learn was characteristic, for it carried with it the gold-headed stick looped into his hand by his little finger.

"The name of her familiar has for the moment escaped me," he said. He had a dry crackling voice which should have been unpleasant but wasn't, I think because it was infused with humour as if there was always a chuckle behind it.

"Walker," I answered. "Christian name Johnnie, I presume."

He laughed aloud at that, a short barking laugh, as his old eyes took in the ridiculous scene. Suddenly his gaze became fixed and I saw that he was staring with particular intensity at a young man who stood slightly apart from the group. The object of the millionaire's attention was a well-made chap on the small side, with a neat head and strong shoulders. Most of the young men in the Dunmanway set looked red and puffy and took their exercise walking from the members' bar to the paddock once a week at the Curragh or in other people's bedrooms later on, but this chap looked hard and tough and fit. I saw Mantovelli's gaze shift from him for a second and meet that of Stuart Jason on the other side of the room. The millionaire gave a slight nod and Jason began to thread his way through the crowd towards him.

Mildred was laughing with an odious young man whose face was the colour it should have been thirty years later. There was nothing for me there. "Don't get too tight, will you, dear," I said to her as I passed. She wasn't tight as it happened and she caught me up in a couple of strides.

"You're outrageous, Simon," she said to me. "Why do you always have to say something unpleasant? I suppose it's because you are so eaten up with self-pity——"

"This is hardly the place to put me on a psychiatrist's couch, is it?"

"Won't you exchange one civil word with my friends?"

"No."

"Why not?"

"Because the only thing that isn't cheap about them is their money."

She took a drink from the glass in her hand. "Look, Simon, I'm through with you——"

"I've realized that for some time, my dear. But do you have to give yourself a stiffener to tell me? Is there brandy in that champagne?"

For an instant I thought that she was going to throw the glass at me and then, presumably, I'd have known. Instead she said, very low: "Damn you. And damn you again." Then she turned on her heel and went back to the young man.

I almost bumped into Maurice. I wondered if he had heard the interchange. It didn't much matter if he had, I supposed. Everyone knew about us, anyway. "Where are the Cézannes, Maurice?" I asked him.

"In the octagon room, I believe. It's across the hall at the back."

The young man who had been the object of our host's attention walked past us as I was turning away.

"Who is that?" I said for I knew that Maurice would know. He is a sort of walking *Tatler*.

"It's easily seen you don't go racing. His name is Roddy Marston. Won the National Hunt Chase at Cheltenham last March and was second in the Gold Cup. He is supposed to be going to be the best G.R. since Harry Brown. That is if the stewards will let him."

"Why won't they? What's wrong with him?"

"He has no visible means of support. Lives with his sister and their uncle, the old General, in Brompton Square. They haven't a bob between them and I don't suppose the old General can give him much. They're distant cousins of mine as it happens."

"Why should Mantovelli be interested in him?"

"Damned if I know. Perhaps he's going to finance him. No, of course that couldn't be."

I took another glass of champagne and went off to find the octagon room.

They were there all right and they were superb. So was the room. It lay right in the heart of the house and it was such a room as only the brothers Adam could have built. Two noble, inlaid mahogany doors gave access to it. Opposite them tall windows showed the view to the terrace and the park and away to the lonely hills. On the walls were the Cézannes.

Far from the party and not regretting it, I stayed there, drinking in the heat and the light, the colour and harshness of those wonderful Provençal landscapes, back by proxy in the cruellest and, for me, the most fascinating country in France. As far as I was concerned anyone could have Cézanne's later pictures, his portraits, still-lifes and the rest. As long as he could make the sun and the heat leap at you, no, more than that, beat out at you from the canvas as he did in those early works, that was enough for me.

"You like those brilliant daubs, Mr. Herald?"

I swung round. He was standing three feet away, watching me, the tiny cup half-way to his lips, the stick hanging from his hand. The cold eyes surveyed me without a shadow of expression in them. The old, lined face was as inscrutable as crocodile skin. How long he had been there I did not know.

But something had made him more aware of me than of just another guest for he had taken the trouble to find out my name. Faintly I felt the first silken, gossamer touch of the web which fate and M. Mantovelli were to weave about me.

"I love Provence," I said simply. "It frightens me but I love it."

"We have tastes in common, it seems."

"I could sit for a day looking at your Cézannes. But why do you hang them here?"

His glance went beyond me through the window and my eyes followed it.

Away in the distance the blue hills lay in the haze. The deep green of the pastures in which the horses grazed stretched out towards them. The sky was flecked, as it almost always is in Ireland, with the dark, black clouds which herald storm and rain.

"I keep them here to remind me of sun and warmth when I am in these cold northern latitudes. Put your stock on that grass and you can see the bone growing in their bodies. But humans—no. Horses and women who love them better than men are the only things which can flourish in this climate. You make a mistake living here, Herald."

"I shouldn't wonder if you weren't right. As it happens I leave for France in a day or two."

"Indeed——"

The door behind us was suddenly flung open and the sound of voices raised in anger came from the room beyond.

"No, I'm damned if I'll take it. Why should I? I can do far better with the American syndicate." It was a young man's voice, high and angry.

"You may never reach the American syndicate."

"Are you threatening me, damn you?"

"No. Warning you."

"You've kept me hanging around long enough with your half-promises, Jason. The deal is off, now and forever. The Americans are going to get it."

"It is a long way from here to Cannes."

"Try and stop me and see what happens—to you or anyone else."

The young man stepped into the room and slammed the heavy door behind him. His face was flushed and his eyes were blazing. He crossed the floor in three strides and went out the further door. He did not notice either of us. It was Roddy Marston, the coming G.R.

CHAPTER 2

Pink Champagne and Barbiturates

"So," Mantovelli said quietly, "you go to France. As it happens, so do I."

The whole incident of the angry young man had not taken more than thirty seconds. Mantovelli went on with the conversation as if it had not taken place at all. But a certain tenseness had come between us and we were both aware of it. He knew that I had heard the strange outburst. I should not have been human if I had not wondered what it all meant. I realized that his conversation was no longer idle talk with a chance acquaintance. Now it was being pursued with an end in view.

"Do you go by car?" he asked.

"Yes," I said. "I'm driving to the Coast."

"Ah. This, of course," he gestured towards the pictures on the walls, "is only a part of my collection. Of all the people here you are the only one who took the trouble to search them out. You must see the rest, Herald. You will pass a night with me in Provence on your way south."

This was more than an invitation; it was an almost unprecedented honour. I heard stories and read gossip paragraphs about the Château Lubenac. It was his retreat. The most precious of his treasures were collected in it and a small army of guards was believed to be on permanent duty there, protecting them. No pictures of the château had ever appeared in the press and one or two enterprising photographers looking for something to sell to the illustrated weeklies had been roughly handled and had had their equipment smashed. Only the millionaire's most intimate friends were entertained there.

Few people, indeed, could say that they knew exactly where it was.

I was as well (if not better) acquainted as most Englishmen with the part of Provence in which it was said to lie, but all I knew for certain was that it was somewhere southeast of Apt, somewhere in that lonely tangle of valleys that is all but uninhabited and almost unexplored.

"You are most kind," I said. I wanted time to think. All my instincts shouted at me not to accept. Danger and fear and violence had come into the room with that young man and still hung there. I was not being invited to spend a night at the Château Lubenac because Mantovelli had suddenly taken a fancy to me. I was neither sufficiently conceited nor sufficiently stupid to believe that. The invitation had been issued because I had heard Roddy Marston kicking up a row. All the stories and whispers about the old man's ruthlessness, his medieval mind and his hired assassins came back to me with a rush. Having got into the Château Lubenac I might not get out again in a hurry.

And yet—I wanted to see the place that so many had tried so hard to enter. I loved houses, I loved Provence, I loved pictures. Here was a chance to see something superb of all three. Besides, my marriage was falling in bits about me, I was on the threshold of middle age and regretting it; I was in the mood and at that stage of life where one wants at least a last fling at the unknown.

"That is indeed good of you," I heard myself saying. "I shall be delighted."

"Very well. My secretary will get in touch with you tomorrow."

For the moment I was dismissed. I wandered back to the party. Mildred was nowhere to be seen. I didn't want any more champagne and it did not seem worth while to go in search of anything else. I went out to the Bentley and drove slowly home.

I didn't expect that Mildred would come back to dinner and, needless to say, she didn't. As it was the cook's night out my solitary meal was a singularly unappetizing one of frazzled cutlets and sodden potatoes. It had begun to rain and a heavy, driving mist was swirling about outside the windows.

Moist and depressing, I thought, as I sipped my claret and looked at the weather and longed for the heat and sunlight of Provence. Well, in a couple of days I should be there. I had been a fool, I supposed, to accept Mantovelli's invitation. Not that it mattered, for I could always change my mind and go on direct to the Coast. But there was no denying the excitement and fascination of the prospect of penetrating to that closely guarded fastness. It would be quite something to see and to say you had seen the Château Lubenac.

I didn't sleep much that night, partly because I had been sleeping badly for ages, partly because I was determined to go abroad and I knew that Mildred was equally determined to stay at home so that I was undoubtedly in for a most crashing row, and partly because I could not get out of my mind the picture of Mantovelli and his old lined face and strange evil eyes, and young Roddy Marston crashing across the room in a fury.

After a third green pill and a great deal of kicking and tossing I did go off into some sort of sleep. It only seemed a minute or so later when the servant came in and pulled the curtains. I was thick in the head, totally unrefreshed and damned liverish. It was still raining. My leg was hurting me a bit, too, as sometimes happened in wet weather.

Mildred didn't appear at breakfast, but that wasn't unusual either. I drank three cups of coffee, chewed some indigestion tablets and felt a bit better, or thought I did.

After breakfast on most days I sit in my study for a while and read the post and *The Times* which comes a day late in Ireland. The letters were on my desk in a neat pile, *The Times*, and the *Autocar* and *Motor Sport* in their wrappers beside them.

Propped up against the little inlaid Chippendale chinaman at the back of the desk was an envelope addressed to me in Mildred's handwriting. Very formal it was—*Simon Herald, Esq., Newlands Abbey, Courtnagay, Co. Kildare.*

I think I knew what was in the letter before I opened it.

She had stuck it long enough she said and now she was off. She didn't suppose that it would make any difference to me. I should go on leading my own life and snarling at everyone to make up for what had gone wrong with it. (She couldn't resist that one.) She didn't suppose, either, that it would interest me to know where she was or what she was doing so she was not leaving any address. She had taken the D.K.W. but she would see that I got it back or was told where to pick it up. There was a lot more which doesn't matter. It was quite a letter.

When I had finished reading it I put it down and looked at the little chinaman. He waved his sword at me and I made a face at him. No doubt he had seen a good many similar situations during the two hundred years of his existence.

It was over, anyway, and over without a final, wretched, humiliating scene. I wondered if she had gone with that ghastly youth from Cork or had merely joined the general cat-house of the Dunmanway crew. I had been in love with her once; at least I supposed I had been. It was rather hard to remember now. It was a pity her yearning to be smart and in the swing had taken her that way. I went on opening my post.

There was a letter from my stockbroker with a transfer for signature, the usual bills and circulars and a typewritten envelope out of which I took a printed card.

I turned the card over in my fingers and looked at it. On its face was a map. With a little pang of excitement I realized that I was looking at directions for getting to the Château Lubenac.

I opened the bookcase above my desk, took out the Michelin Sheet for the area and unfolded it. Then I placed the card over the map. It was simple enough once you had the card to point out the way. You went along N.100 to Apt; then you bore into the hills. The château itself was indeed remote, quite lost in that tangle of mountains and valleys.

On the back of the card was the typewritten message: *M. Mantovelli will expect you on the afternoon of the 6th.* Well, there was nothing to keep me now. Certainly I would see the inside of Mantovelli's retreat, admire his pictures and drink his great wines. And there was no one to care if I never came out again.

I picked up the telephone and made a call to Clevedon Court.

"Tell M. Mantovelli", I said to the secretary who answered it, "that I am looking forward to seeing him on the 6th."

Pink Champagne and Barbiturates

Three days later I was eating my dinner in Le Vieux Fort in Villeneuve Les Avignon.

Once I had closed up the house and got myself under way I had come far and come fast. And in the back of my mind was the feeling that I had been followed all the way. I hadn't bothered about it. It might, of course, have been imagination but, after all, if Mantovelli wanted to make sure of my presence what more likely than that he would have kept me under observation?

I had turned on my tracks once and had seen a flash of red as a big car swung suddenly into a side road. In Lyons I had driven round the city before taking the way to the south. But a sleek red Ferrari had picked me up a few miles out. I reduced my pace to an amble and he came near enough for me to see him quite clearly in my mirror. I accelerated and, although he had the legs of me, he never passed me. Whatever I did there he sat, just the regulation distance behind me. It might have been coincidence, it might have been imagination; but I didn't think so. I fancied that one of the Mantovelli enterprises owned that car. I wouldn't have minded owning it myself.

It was cool in the evenings as it is in early June and dinner was set inside. I had the table by the window and was eating *asperges en vinaigre*, superb and succulent and tender to the roots. Outside the Rhône swept past and the Palais Des Papes gleamed in its floodlighting. I had an *entrecôte* steak that melted in my mouth—the food in Le Vieux Fort is as good as anywhere in France—finished my Côtes du Rhône and wandered out on to the terrace.

The wine had not relaxed me as I had hoped it would. I felt as tired as all get out, and as tight strung as a violin string. And I knew that I was not going to sleep. There was a little bottle full of green pills upstairs and another of yellow ones. They were supposed to make me sleep and they were about as much use as a long drink of lemonade. As far as I could see all they did was to leave me feeling like hell in the mornings.

Besides, I had to face it, I was lonely. Mildred and I had been married for nearly seven years and I had got used to having someone around if only for part of the time, someone to talk to even if it was just to have a row. The thought of going to bed alone in a strange room and tossing and turning and getting nearer and nearer to climbing the walls every minute was more than I could face.

I went out to where the car was parked under the limes, drove slowly over the Pont St. Benedict and into Avignon itself. My idea was to have a few *fines* and see what they could do to help me and at any rate to kill a few hours of the night. I parked the car in front of the Palais and walked slowly down towards the Place de L'Orloge.

As I turned the corner by the Banque de France a girl came pelting around it, looking over her shoulder as she ran. She hit me head on and all but sent me flying. I grabbed first her and then the railings and ended, still upright, with my arm around her.

"That's done it," she gasped. "He's got me. Look out!"

He was a big chap and he came after her full tilt, his arm outstretched.

Quite instinctively I stuck out my leg. He met it in mid-career and I think the first thing that hit the ground was his chin. As he went I caught a glimpse of his face in the lamplight. "Oh!" she said. "He'll kill us now. Get me away from here—please."

"I'm not too anxious to stay myself," I answered. "Come on." I grabbed her by the wrist and ran for the Bentley.

"We can't go back past him," she said as I started the engine.

"We're not going to," I replied. I swung the car into the little street by the curio shop, shot down the hill and turned sharp right. I thanked my stars I knew my way. Three minutes later I was pulling up in the cobbled court-yard of Le Vieux Fort.

"We seem awfully near," she said nervously. "Will he find us?"

"He's only just beginning to realize what hit him. Come in and have a *fine*. If you don't need one I do."

They had put on the terrace lights. As we sat down I looked at her properly for the first time. She was young, though not quite so young as I had thought. Her hair was a mixture of brown and auburn and, unruly now, ran in a mass of curls round her head. She had a short, straight nose, a mouth that looked made for love and laughing and a well-shaped chin with a hint of character in it. She was wearing a plain white blouse and a coloured skirt with slashed pockets and a flare to it. Altogether she was a very attractive girl and a most disturbing apparition for an old gentleman of forty who is trying to forget his marriage.

When the drinks were in front of us I saw that she was shivering. "Cold?" I asked.

"No," she said. "Frightened."

"I see. Well, sip that slowly. It will do you good."

She said nothing until the *fine* was gone and I made no move to break the silence. Then, "Thanks," she said.

"Can I help?" I asked.

She was silent for a little while. Then, "It's not fair to drag you into it," she said slowly.

"I'm not at all certain that I'm not in it a bit already.

That chap who was chasing you was Stuart Jason."

She pushed back her chair and started to stand up. "You're one of them!" she exclaimed.

I reached over and pushed her gently down into the chair again. "No, I'm not. I'm an elderly party called Simon Herald who was at a rout given by a certain M. Mantovelli a few nights ago. I overheard a conversation I was not supposed to hear between Jason and a young man called Marston. I gather Jason is in charge of Mantovelli's dirty work. Now, does that help?"

She looked at me, wondering whether to trust me or not.

"You might as well take a chance on me," I said. "There doesn't seem to be much other help around."

She hesitated still. And then, suddenly, it all came out in a rush. "It's not altogether that," she said. "But these people—they're something I never thought really existed. They are evil. It is like dreaming that you are mixed up in a gangster film and then waking up and finding that you are not dreaming at all. And Jason—I think he fell in love with violence during the war and can't forget it. And, oh I know it sounds awful, but you did say it yourself—you aren't all that young, are you?"

I'd asked for it, but even so it nicked me. "I may have one foot in the grave," I said. "But the other can still kick—or trip. But thanks for the thought."

She shivered again and her teeth closed over her lower lip. A waiter put two more *fines* in front of us. I pushed one across the table to her. "Try that," I said. "It does help."

She swallowed some of the spirit and put the glass down. Then she looked at me again, appraisingly. I could read her thoughts as plainly as if she had spoken them. She was sizing me up, trying to decide whether I was of the stuff that could be any real help or not.

"Cheer up," I said. "I used to be moderately tough before gin and the world caught up with me. You might as well tell all."

She coloured. "Oh," she said. "I do seem to be doing this awfully badly. And you have been kind——"

I smiled at her again. She was easy to smile at and, rather to my surprise, I found myself hoping that there was some way in which I could help her. When you get to my age you can usually tell by looking at them the nice girls from the tramps, and she looked a genuinely nice girl. And there hadn't been many genuinely nice girls round me lately.

"I'm Sue Marston, Roddy's sister," she said.

"I see. That puts you into it all right, whatever it is." I hadn't much liked the look of that young man. He had seemed too sure of himself altogether. But I had wondered what he was up to. Now, apparently, I was going to find out.

"Roddy has got hold of something Mantovelli wants. Jason tried to buy it from him for Mantovelli in London. Roddy wouldn't sell. He said they weren't giving him enough. There is an American syndicate who, he says, will give him more. He is in Cannes now, dealing with them."

"What is this thing?"

"I don't know. But it must be valuable, enormously valuable. You see, I don't know if you race at all, but Roddy is an amateur rider. He is awfully good. They say that he is right in the first class already and this was his first full season. But he hasn't any money—or at least he hasn't enough to satisfy the stewards that he can live without racing. You have to do that, you know. He says that if he can sell the thing he won't have any worries left and the stewards can go to hell."

"Why doesn't he turn pro if he is as good as that? This is a democratic day and age or so I've heard."

"It's difficult to explain if you don't go racing, but everybody has told him that he should do at least another season as an amateur. If he turns now he won't get the rides. It's hard enough to get them when you turn anyway and in a way he is still only promising. He's only just lost the allowance. If he did well in another season he could turn when he was on the top. There is a shortage of good pro's. He is tremendously ambitious."

"I see, or think I do. Where do you come in?"

"I flew out and met him in Avignon. There was no one else he could trust, he said. I'm to meet him again to-morrow in the Hotel de L'Éperon in Arles."

"What for?"

"I've got the thing he wants to sell."

"Good God! That's why Jason was after you. How did they find out?"

"They are terrifyingly efficient. I suppose they followed me all the way. Two of them just grabbed me in the street. They were taking me to a car. Then I suddenly remembered something I'd read in a thriller. I trod on the nearest man's instep as hard as I could and ran."

I laughed. "That must have shaken them a bit," I said. "How do you know so much about Jason?"

"I met him in London when they were trying to get Roddy to sell. He came to the house. He took me out to try to get me on his side. Look, please, couldn't we go somewhere away from here for a bit, anyway? I feel as if he were just behind me all the time."

"All right. Come on." She was to meet her brother in Arles tomorrow. She might as well go there now.

I led the way out to the car. When she saw it she gave

me a mischievous look. "Why," she said. "It's a Bentley. I hadn't time to look before. It is a bit middle-aged, isn't it? Roddy has a T.R.3."

"I hope he can drive it," I said. We slid over the cobbles, up the steep hill where the open culvert is, out of the village and across the river. I drove round the ramparts, turned right for St. Remy, and settled down to let her go. The limes lining the road by the Rhône gradually closed up in the headlights as the speed mounted. Avignon fell behind. I kept an eye on the driving mirror. No lights came into it and stayed there. We were clear.

"He can't pick us up?" she asked nervously.

"No," I said. "How can he check every car that goes through Avignon at night? Even if he could he couldn't catch us—despite the advanced age of the car and its driver." I didn't tell her about the red Ferrari and tried to dismiss it from my own mind. But I kept my eye on the mirror.

"Where are we going?" she asked in rather subdued tones.

"To Arles," I said. "To see some other ruins."

We cleared St. Remy without incident and ran up the long slope past the remains of Glanum and the triumphal arch. I began to relax. I was sure now that we were not followed. "Tell me some more about Jason," I said as we entered the cleft in the Alpilles. "I think I remember something about him from the war. Wasn't he in the 44th?"

"Yes, and he did frightfully well in the Desert. He got a double D.S.O. and an M.C. He likes war, he likes hurting people and he likes killing. That is the only way I can describe him. There was some frightful trouble, just at the end, in Germany. It was about torturing werwolves,

I think. Roddy knows all about it. Jason would have been court-martialled only that General, I forget his name, Roddy says they are two of a kind, got it hushed up. He left the army after the war. I think he was told he would never get any further. Then he lost all his money racing. He had a wife and she left him. When Mantovelli picked him up he was penniless and living on his friends. Now he wants to get back at the world for what it has done to him or for what he thinks it has done to him. Every time he injures someone or gets the better of them or hurts them in any way he gets a vicious satisfaction. He really is evil. He's attractive, too, in a beastly sort of way. Don't let's talk any more about him."

I thought of him as we drove on through that haunted, secret countryside, that queer, handsome, arrogant death's head of a face on that splendid body. I remembered, now, stories I had heard during the war and after it and I wondered, as I often wondered, what it was that shaped us as we are. In Jason's case was it some congenital flaw in his character, or was it some external pressure, something that marked him as he grew that made the evil in him overshadow the rest? Was I really, as Mildred said I was, eaten up with self-pity, consumed with a determination never to let myself enjoy anything since that night at Le Mans nearly ten years ago now? Did all my complaints, my wretchedness, my sleeplessness, my ulcers real or imaginary come from a refusal to accept the cards I had been dealt? Possibly. But Mildred in many ways, let's face it, was a bitch of the first water, and had she been different I might have been different too. I realized I was beginning to institute a self-pitying jag and shoved the whole parcel of thoughts away from me. I looked at the girl in the other seat. She was curled up like a child, fast asleep.

Pink Champagne and Barbiturates

The Hotel de L'Éperon was in a side street near the arena. It wasn't much of a hotel and I wondered where young Marston had found it. Not in the Guide Michelin at any rate, I decided.

The door was shut when we arrived. I hammered on it with my fist and put my thumb on the bell and kept it there. After some time it was opened by a greasy-looking chap in his shirt sleeves, rubbing the sleep out of his eyes.

Inside was a dingy hall floored with cracked pink tiles. A wooden clap-board counter with a key-rack behind it was against one wall. At the far end were narrow stone stairs. There was nothing in the way of furniture except a dark oak bench.

"Yes," the clerk said from the door where he was looking sideways at Sue and the car, he had a room for the night, one room only, a double room. I had reckoned for this coming over in the car for I knew that no French hotel can on any occasion offer a mixed couple anything other than a double room. The desk clerk's smirk confirmed my opinion that I should not get a room to myself in the Hotel de L'Éperon. We had not been followed; there could not be much risk in leaving her though I had hoped for something better than this third-rate place. I walked past the clerk and out to the car. "I've got a room for you," I said.

She looked younger and more defenceless than ever as she stood in that sleazy hall. I paid the deposit on the room and collected the key. The clerk put his elbows on the counter and looked at us with open interest and speculation. He was wideawake now and taking it all in. His eyes were cunning, greedy and knowing, the eyes of a bad servant on the make, the sort of eyes you see in that sort of hotel.

I hated leaving her there. Short of sleeping with her there was nothing I could do about it, and I didn't want to sleep with her—or, to be honest, I did, I suppose, but not in those particular circumstances.

She was standing at the bottom of the stairs, her hands thrust into the big pockets of her skirt. "I'm frightened," she said simply. "It's Jason. He terrifies me. You're sure he didn't follow us?"

"Certain. Look—it's only for a night. Your brother is coming tomorrow, isn't he?"

She nodded. "Yes, I know but——" Her glance took in the hall and the desk and she shivered.

I crossed to the desk, and took out a thousand-franc note. "Are you sure you haven't a room?" I said.

The clerk looked hungrily at the note. Then he cast his eyes down and rubbed his sleeve along the boards of the counter. "No, M'sieu, it is the last."

At any rate I'd tried. I went back to her. "I'll ring you first thing tomorrow," I said. "If you feel jumpy shove a chair under the door handle as well as locking it. But, look here, there is no necessity. No one knows you are here."

She shivered again. She was very alone, poor kid. She wanted to be held and warmed and reassured, to have someone to turn to, someone who would take over in this ghastly dream she was living. I nearly weakened for I, too, wanted company and sympathy. I took a step forward and our eyes met. We both knew what was there between us, what the urgency of the moment held for us. And that knowledge brought me up short. "No," I said. "No. It won't go. We'd hate each other for ever."

"Please take this, then, and keep it for me. It's what I have for Roddy. What he wants to sell them. I know I oughtn't to ask you, but I can't, I can't keep it any longer."

She took a short, flat envelope out of her pocket and thrust it into my hand. Before I could say anything she had turned and gone quickly upstairs.

I waited until I heard her door shut and the key turn in the lock. Then I went out to the car. The clerk's eyes followed me all the way to the door.

There was a café open in the Place Lamartine on the way out. I pulled up there and ordered a *fine à l'eau*. I hadn't realized how tired I was and it was a long way back to Avignon. When the drink was in front of me I took out the envelope which she had given me and looked at it. It was a thick, tough manilla envelope rather battered and worn and heavily sealed at the back. There were no markings on it of any kind. I turned it over in my hands. There was no clue to its contents and I could not begin to guess what they were. If it was valuable enough to have caused all this commotion I supposed I ought to do something about keeping it safe.

I had recognized Jason. It was at least possible that he had recognized me. Tomorrow, he might be coming after me in Avignon. Perhaps he was even now waiting for me in the Vieux Fort. It was unlikely, but it was possible. I looked again at the envelope lying on the white-topped table in front of me. What the hell was I to do with it? And then I had an idea.

An aunt of mine lived near Aix. She was pretty eccentric, my Aunt Dorothy. She had lived for years in one of the remote villages of Haute Provence, just why no one in the family ever knew. There, to protect her, she bought a man-eating cross-bred Alsatian called Baskerville. Finally the village of Sorgne had proved too lonely and savage even for her and she had moved to Aix bringing

Baskerville with her to terrify the neighbourhood and to cost her a small fortune in compensation.

But she and her dog still retained the distrust of strangers engendered by their years in the mountains. It occurred to me that Roddy Marston's envelope, whatever was in it, would be a long sight safer with my Aunt Dorothy at the moment than with me.

I sent for ink and writing paper and another *fine*. When they came I wrote a few lines to my aunt telling her to keep the enclosure in a particularly safe place for me while I was on holiday in France. I added my regards to Baskerville and sealed the whole lot up. Then I got back into the car, posted the letter and headed back for Avignon.

The moon was rising as I drove out through the newly laid rice fields and past the great bleached bulk of Montmajour. Now, sitting behind the big, whispering engine and trying to let the car drive itself, I had time to realize just how tired I was. The only thing that was keeping me going was the brandy and that was dying in me every mile. Between Fontvieille and Paradoux I turned left on to D.78. I couldn't remember the road very well but I had an idea that this way saved some miles. Anyway when you are playing the sort of game in which I seemed most reluctantly to have got engaged it is always as well to return a different way from the one you set out.

Running up through the Vallon de la Fontaine underneath the wrecked and twisted houses of Les Baux my resolution to get back to Avignon failed me. I was whacked and I knew it and I remembered the hotel at the head of the valley.

Leaving the car in the forecourt I walked in through the little gate. The water in the pool gleamed silver in the moonlight; beside it two expensive-looking types with stomachs were drinking champagne with two expensive-looking blondes. A third was standing by the pool in a white bathing dress. She didn't look as if she'd require very much persuasion to take it off.

They had a room for me and I told them to send up my bags, a bottle of Vichy and a bottle of their champagne *rosé*. The latter I knew I was going to regret but I had a raging thirst, I wanted something which would mix with the cognac I had been drinking and I still have a schoolboy fondness for pink champagne.

There was a vast and luxurious-looking bed—if anything was going to make me sleep I supposed it would—some Provençal furniture and a telephone. While they were bringing up my luggage and the ice-buckets I picked up the handset and told them to get me through to the Hotel de L'Éperon at Arles.

I didn't bother about the wine-glass; I sloshed the tooth-mug full of the wine and drank it off. I was as keyed up as all get-out and I couldn't sit still. My sleeping pills were in a little leather travelling medicine case. Unzipping this I had a look at them. I had quite forgotten what you were supposed to do with the green and what with the yellow, but I knew something akin to a Mickey Finn was needed to knock me out that night. I compromised by taking two yellow and a green, like a sandwich, and had another swig at the champagne.

Then the call came through.

There weren't, it appeared, telephones in the rooms at the Hotel de L'Éperon so the clerk could not connect me with Mademoiselle—unless, of course, he went up and got her. I could almost see him smacking his lips. I gave him my number and told him to tell her to ring me if she wanted me.

Then I had a shot at sleep.

Nothing happened. I hadn't had much hope that it would. The sheets felt as if they were on fire. I twisted and turned. My head was too low; I piled up the pillows then it was too high so I threw them away. Every time I thought I had achieved sleep something came along and prodded me awake again. I pulled the curtains to shut out the moon and opened them to let in the air. I finished the champagne and took another green pill to level things up. It didn't do any good.

When I had given up all hope of ever sleeping again a great hand came from somewhere, caught hold of me and rammed my roaring head down towards oblivion. Buzzing noises sounded in my ears. It was like going over the Alexandra Falls in a bucket. Then I went to sleep if you can call it that.

CHAPTER 3

Roman Ruins

I was still underneath the Alexandra Falls—at least I
supposed I was for the roaring in my ears must have
been the roaring of falling water. But someone had got
hold of me and was trying to pull me out. Someone had
me by the arm and was shaking it none too gently. In fact
it wasn't being shaken, it was being wrenched. I woke up.
It was like coming out of an anaesthetic. Come to think of
it I suppose that is what it was.

Roddy Marston was bending over me, a scowl on his
young face.

"What have you done with her?" he said. "I ought to
break you in bits."

My head was still singing and banging. I ran a hand
over my eyes to try to get them open and pushed myself
up on the pillows.

"I don't know how you got here," I said. "But you
can get the hell out of my room until you learn to keep a
civil tongue in your head."

He scowled at me again but he took a step back from the
bed. "Where is Sue?" he said in a more reasonable tone
of voice.

"I left her last night in a perfectly bloody pub in Arles
called the Hotel de L'Éperon. Apparently you found it for
her. I don't think much of your choice."

"She's not there now."

"What?"

"A man called for her a few hours ago and she went off with him. That's what the clerk told me. He said she had come in late last night with someone who later phoned from this number."

"And you didn't bother to check up whether it was the same man who called for her but came rushing over here with fire in your eyes. You are a damned young fool." I looked at my watch. It was eight o'clock. I had the world's most Godawful barbiturate hangover and no wonder. I couldn't have been asleep more than a couple of hours. "Get on to the telephone and order up some *petit déjeuner*," I told him.

Jason had evidently got on to her trail and picked her up. The thought of it and her terror of him made me feel slightly sick. Pushing aside the covers I got out of bed. My head was like a lump of scrap iron, old and very battered. I opened the Vichy and drank half a tumblerful; then I put my head and shoulders underneath the cold tap. After three minutes of this I began to register again. "Did you leave any loose ends lying around in Cannes?" I asked him as I shaved. "If you did, that is where they found out the hotel in Arles was your rendezvous."

"It's my business what I did in Cannes," he snapped back. "All I want from you is to tell me what has happened to Sue."

"Stuart Jason has got her. That's what has happened to her," I said brutally. "And what is more I think you deserve the hiding of your young life for getting her into this." I was pouring scalding coffee down my throat and spreading butter and greengage jam on to my *brioches*. Life was coming back to me every minute.

We glared mutual dislike at each other across the breakfast tray.

"I'd like to see you do it," he said looking at me scornfully.

"Twenty years ago I'd have had a damn good shot at it."

He sat there, hard and handsome and young and over-confident. Old and battered as I was I almost went into a lost battle. Then I told myself that we were in a tight enough fix or, rather, Sue was, and fisticuffs in a hotel room weren't going to solve anything for anyone—except myself perhaps.

"Listen," I said, putting down my cup. "I don't like you any more than you like me but unfortunately for both of us we are in this together now. I got your sister out of a spot of bother in Avignon last night and took her to Arles. She was frightened and she gave me your ruddy envelope to keep for her. Any moment now Jason and his precious crew are going to find out that she hasn't got it and the whole lot of them are going to come after me—and you too."

"Give me that envelope," he said through set teeth.

"I haven't got it."

"Where is it?"

"I'll decide later whether I tell you that."

"If you don't tell me I'll beat it out of you right now."

"Listen, you young pup, one more crack like that and I'll sit here and wait for Jason and I'll tell him where it is. Anything I'm doing now I'm doing for your sister and her safety. I don't give a damn about you or your precious envelope. Is that clear?"

We went down to the car with an electric silence between us.

This time I went straight up the hill and through the defile underneath the ruined château. Then I turned right on to the road which runs through the plain below Les Baux. I reckoned if they were coming for me they would obviously come the shorter route and anyway the same instinct which had urged me last night again told me not to use the same road twice.

In the car young Marston thawed a bit. He reckoned he'd been a bit rough, he said. But he was upset. If I'd saved Sue he supposed he should thank me. He had left a forwarding address in his hotel at Cannes. That must have been how they had found the Hotel de L'Éperon. He had hired a car and come over to Les Baux and now, please, where was the envelope?

I'd been thawing a bit myself. After all the thing wasn't my property. "I sent it to an aunt of mine in Aix to look after," I said. "I'll get it back for you. But first of all we'd better see if we can pick up any traces of your sister in Arles."

"What do you think they'll do to her?"

"Nothing much, I imagine. They'll use her as a hostage once they find out that she has not got the envelope. What is it anyway?"

"Only three people in the world know that. Myself, Mantovelli and the head of the American syndicate. I'm not telling anyone else."

"That's all right by me. It is your affair, not mine."

When we came to the junction where I had turned off last night some sixth sense warned me to slow. It was just as well I did.

A mile away in the clear air I saw the sun flash on something red on the road. I put my foot on the brake and drew to a standstill.

"What's wrong?" he asked.

I doubted if they were coming our way for they were

almost certain to take the direct road. Even so I would
have felt happier if I had had a gun. Then I heard the song
of the gear change and knew I had guessed right.

The red Ferrari came into plain view. Driven on a lovely
line it swung into D.78 without pause or hesitation and
snarled out of sight.

"They're after us," I said. "I thought so. We haven't
much time. That fellow can drive," I added as an after-
thought as I let in the clutch.

We parked the car by the Arena and walked down the
street towards the hotel. The heat was blinding by now,
that stifling all-enveloping heat which beats up out of the
Camargue and leaves you limp and listless.

"Let me do the talking," I said as we went in the door.

The same clerk was on duty. They didn't give him much
rest. He either couldn't or wouldn't tell us much. A man
had come with a message from Mademoiselle's brother.
She had let him into her room and they had gone out together. That was all the clerk would say.

"You stay here," I told Marston. "I'm going upstairs.
Keep an eye on this insect."

The clerk tried to protest. I knocked his hand aside and
took down the key.

The room had not been made up but there was nothing
there for me. I took it to pieces. I stripped the bedclothes,
turned over the pillows, pulled out the drawers, but there
was no message, nothing to indicate what had happened
four hours ago in that dingy apartment. It had been a for-
lorn hope anyway. I went downstairs again.

"Not a thing," I said in response to Marston's look. "I
wonder if we could beat anything else out of him?" I
nodded at the clerk. He was standing by the door.

He left the door and came over to us. "You found nothing to help you, M'sieu?" he said to me. "Can I get M'sieu anything now?" He was being obsequiously helpful. His attitude had changed altogether too quickly. There was a hint of triumph in his smile. Two strides took me to the door.

The red Ferrari was just entering the street.

"They're here," I said. "I knew that fellow could drive but I didn't think he was as good as that. We'll get out the back."

"What shall we do with this?" he nodded at the clerk.

"You're the strongarm man. Take care of him."

He did it with quickness and efficiency. His feet slid across the tiled floor; his left went out and then his right. They did not appear to do more than flicker. The clerk's head snapped backwards. His eyes went up and I caught him as he fell. The speed of it was blinding.

In so far as I was capable of thinking of anything except getting out of that place I registered a vote of thanks to myself for not mixing it with young Marston in that hotel room. Even twenty years ago I wouldn't have lasted five seconds. He was quite out of my class.

"Very neat," I said. "Have you broken his jaw?"

He gave me a half grin. "I learnt to fight at Leatherby's," he said. "I had to."

"Come on. Quick!" I got the unconscious man by the collar and lugged him along by the heels. He weighed nothing at all.

There was a door behind the counter. A short, flagged passage led us into another room. It was a noisome kitchen, and it was empty. The stench of garlic was overpowering. At the back of the fireplace a dark opening showed a flight of steps going down to a cellar.

"In there with him," I said. We pitched him down the

steps and slammed and bolted the door. "Now—out."

Another door brought us into a tiny, rectangular yard. The wall was only four feet high. Once over this we were in an alleyway.

The mouth of the alley gave into the street alongside the hotel. There were as yet no sounds or noises of pursuit.

Beside the hotel the red Ferrari was drawn up. It was unattended; in all probability it was also unlocked. I took the keys of the Bentley out of my pocket and handed them to him.

"They'll be after us in a minute," I said. "Even with a start that thing has the legs of us. Cut back to the car and wait for me."

"What are you going to do?"

"Put the Ferrari out of action—if I can."

As casually as I could I sauntered down the street towards the low red car. There was no one in the doorway of the hotel, and no sounds came from within. They must still be searching. But pretty soon they must find him.

I put my hand on the driver's door. It was already warm in the sun. The door opened to my pull.

No one took any notice of me. I was just another driver opening the door of his car.

I freed the bonnet, jerked it up and looked at the maze of machinery inside. An old trick that we used to play at weddings when we were young came to my mind and it only took me a moment or two to put it into practice. Then I slammed the bonnet shut and was off up the street.

When I had covered twenty yards I started to run. The heat seemed to come up out of the stones of that narrow street and hit me. In ten paces I was pouring sweat and gasping.

Marston was nearing the Bentley when I turned into the

Roman Ruins

Place de la Major. I was just in time to see the men come round from behind the car and make for him. Behind me I thought I heard a shout. I hadn't run like this for years. I tried to put on speed. The heat in the Place was stifling.

The men were in blue Provençal jackets and trousers. One of them was huge, a great, burly brute. He had what looked like a short iron bar in his hand. The smaller man outdistanced him and got to Marston first. This was something he had cause to regret.

Marston saw him coming, and waited for him. Then he cut him in pieces. Only the big fellow was in the fight when I came up. He came straight for me. He looked the size of a mountain. The old walls of the Arena loomed over us. It had seen this sort of thing before.

"It's as good a place as any to say *moritus te saluto*," I remarked and I hit the big fellow as hard as I could in the stomach. It was like hitting a brick wall and about as effective.

I didn't see the iron bar until the instant before it got me. With a desperate lurch I managed to throw myself to one side. It shaved my head and went into my shoulder with a thud.

We had worked over almost to the steps and, ultimately, that is what saved me. Marston came up with a run and went boring into the big thug. He hit him and hit him again. The thug grunted in pain and swung the bar. Marston slid under it with the grace and timing of a ballet dancer. His left went in and out and I could hear the smack of its impact. The thug took a pace backwards. He was on the very edge of the steps; his foot met air and he went over and down like a falling factory chimney. Together we turned and ran for the car.

"You drive," I said as we reached it. "He's got me on the shoulder."

He put her into gear with a crash and dived into the maze of streets behind the Arena.

"I suppose you know where you are going?" I asked him as we took a corner with two wheels across the pavement.

"Haven't a clue."

"Well for Christ's sake take it steady or we'll be Roman remains ourselves."

We grazed two bicycles and missed the side of an ancient Renault by inches. Its driver's remarks on our ancestry sizzled through the burning air. By this time I wasn't too sure where we were myself but his driving was frightening me more than the big thug had done five minutes ago, which is saying something. I moved my shoulder to see if I could take over. A stab of pain shot through me. That was enough. I couldn't. I had to leave it to him.

"Where are we heading for?" he asked.

"Aix, if we ever get there with you at the wheel. You'd better have your property back. And I want to get my aunt out of this. I shouldn't have got her into it."

"Won't we be followed?"

I laughed. "Not unless they can work out the Ferrari rotation of cylinders quicker than I think they can," I said. "I switched the plug leads."

For the first time in our short acquaintance he looked at me with something less than contempt in his glance.

"How the devil——" he began.

We all but hit a *camion* coming out of a side street. The subsequent swerve missed a pompous-looking Englishman at the wheel of a parked Daimler by just about his paintwork and no more. Their voices added to the general protest on our progress.

"Don't you know to keep your eyes on your right?" I said. "Turn here—if you can."

He got her around without any more trouble and passed an *agent* without getting me arrested. To my relief I saw the walls of the Place de la République coming up. I knew where we were now. Two minutes later we were in the traffic on the Boulevard des Lices and heading for Aix.

"I hate to say this to you for I don't know what will happen," I said. "But let her go a bit now—if you can."

The first part of that road is neither easy nor fast and I was soon regretting what I had said. Within a minute I knew that although he might be the most promising amateur rider in England he had little or no idea how to handle a fast car.

I have heard it said by people who ought to know better that a man who is good on a horse or in an aeroplane will automatically be a master behind the wheel of a car. It's utter balls, of course. The things are completely different. Some of the brilliant horsemen I've known in Ireland or in my regiment were criminals in a car. A feeling for horse-flesh is not at all the same thing as a feeling for machinery. Even hands on a horse are different from hands in a car.

Here beside me was a living example of the truth of what I was thinking. He had about as much judgment of *pace* as a sixteen-year-old schoolgirl and no idea at all how to take a line and hold it. At the present moment he was scarcely fit to be let loose on the public with a pre-war Austin seven and I told him so.

The road was lousy with huge lorries thundering through the heat. It always is.

"For God's sake mind these *camions*," I said to him. "They'll crowd you if you give them half a chance. No, don't try to take him now. You haven't got either the road or the revs. DON'T, I said. Damn you, didn't you hear me?"

He slammed on the brakes at the last minute and I found myself with my face in the windscreen staring at the exhaust of a ten-ton truck.

"And you have a T.R.3," I said, as I picked myself out of the fascia. "I'm sorry for it."

The trouble was that one half of me was enjoying all this. I had found something that he couldn't do well, something that gave me a weapon with which to crack his self-confidence. Basically, I suppose, it was all bound up with the fact that I was middle-aged and a failure while he was young and on the threshold of success.

The other half of me was not enjoying it at all. Apart altogether from the exhibition of ghastly driving and the ill-treatment being handed out to my car it was just possible that they might manage to restart the Ferrari. And that artist who drove it, whoever he was, would have little trouble overhauling us with young Marston at the wheel.

Where the road runs broad and black and straight across the yellow waste of La Crau I thought that even he had a chance of making time. All he had to do was to sit still, let her go and pass the *camions* when and where he had room. But he could not do it without risking our necks. I think most of the trouble was that he had never before sat behind a big engine at speed or tried to control a big wheelbase. And, say what you like, driving a Bentley is a bit different from driving one of those high-revving sports cars. In horsey parlance I imagine it's rather the same as the sudden promotion from a hunter to a racehorse.

After the cross where you turn off for Martigues we came on an immense *camion* going our way. It was towing a trailer almost as big as itself. Behind the trailer was a Renault *quatre chevaux* on a rigid tow-bar banging about like a dinghy behind a yacht. The whole thing was practically a convoy in itself and took up a fair amount of room on the road.

Young Marston was doing a steady eighty.

He pulled out to pass on a blind uphill rise. We missed the oncoming *camion* by twenty feet at the most.

When I got my breath back, "Pull up," I said. "I'm going to take her."

"You can't. What about your shoulder?"

"I could drive better than you with both hands behind my back. Pull up."

With a very sulky look on his face he pulled the car into the side of the road. I slid across behind the wheel. The heat came up off the tarmac in shimmering lines. It burnt at you from the harsh yellow grass of the wasteland. It was like being surrounded by the air from a furnace. Forty yards from us two *camions* had pulled in and their crews were asleep under the shelter of some scrubby trees. Sensible chaps, I thought.

I moved my shoulder gently. It still hurt but it seemed easier. I would use it as little as possible. No red Ferrari appeared in the mirror. I pulled out and put down my foot. The needle came round the dial in a gentle steady arc. I slid her into top at seventy and took two *camions* as they came without check or fuss. "That's how daddy does it," I said.

"You needn't be so bloody," he said sulkily. "Everyone isn't able to drive like a racing crack."

"No? Everyone isn't able to ride winners, either. You needn't be so bloody about that."

"I'm not bloody about it."

"It strikes me you are. You don't think anyone really worth your while except those who ride with you now or

who rode with the best when they could." He didn't
answer this but scowled out through the windscreen. "It
gave you the hell of a shock to be hauled by the scruff of
the neck out of the driving seat of this car," I went on,
determined to rub it in. "I suppose it is the first time in
your life you've been told you do something damn badly."

"I might have managed it if you hadn't been cursing
me all the time. Anyway, who the hell wants to go in for
fancy driving. Cars are only conveyances——"

"But not antique and useless ones like horses. I thought
that was it. It's just what I have said. You think too much
of yourself to learn how to drive. It's not a gentleman's
pursuit, is it, like steeplechasing or boxing?"

"I had to learn to fight at Leatherby's to survive."

"I saw plenty like you in the war, young feller-me-lad.
They wouldn't get out of the saddle and into a tank, and
then they complained when accountants and bank clerks
and wine merchants passed them by and came back wearing
the gongs they thought they should have had."

"I wasn't in the war."

"Don't let that worry you. Your kind haven't changed
since the Crimea."

We drove on through the heat, hating each other.

My aunt's villa was outside Aix, in the rolling countryside around the Aqueduct de Rocquefavour. I turned off at
the aerodrome, partly to confound the pursuit, if there was
any, and partly because in my opinion the way through
Miramas and by the Lac de Berre is the more direct route,
and, anyway, you avoid the *camions*.

My shoulder was not all that bad. Sometimes when I
moved it quickly the stab of pain came, and I could not do
much with my arm. Apart from that it was not giving me
trouble; but everything else was catching up on me a bit.

After all, I'd had a heavy twenty-four hours. Rescuing a young woman in distress, being woken out of a barbiturate haze by an angry young man and brawling in the Arena at Arles in the heat of the Midi is not at all what I am accustomed to on a Continental holiday.

I suppose it was the result of all this but the heat, which does not usually affect me at all, was quite definitely getting at me now. I wanted to open my mouth and pant like a dog, my tongue was dry and the skin on my face was pulling tight. I didn't like it, especially as every now and then the landscape around me started to blur and swim. As we went past the tall fencing of the munitions factory, to take my mind off things in general I began to chant to myself. It was a silly adaptation of Chesterton which had been running through my head for several days in the way these things will. I had quite forgotten that Marston was sitting beside me which in itself is an indication of the state I was in.

"'*Mr. Mantovelli the millionaire,*'" I chanted. "'*He wouldn't have wine or wife, he couldn't endure complexity; he lived the simple life. He ordered his lunch by megaphone in manly, simple tones, and used all his motors for canvassing voters, and twenty telephones——*'"

"I say. Are you all right?" Marston's voice interrupted me and brought me back to where I was. It also brought home to me the fact that we were going through Miramas and that I felt extremely unwell.

"Of course I am."

"Well, you don't sound it. What is all that about Mantovelli?"

"It's a little hymn to the good rich man. '*Mr. Mantovelli was most refined and quietly, neatly dressed, say all the American newspapers that know refinement best; and not, as anyone would expect, a Tiger Skin, all striped and specked, and a Peacock Hat with the tail erect, a scarlet tunic with sunflowers decked, that might have had a more marked effect—'* " I chuckled. "It might, too," I said. "Describes him, doesn't it?"

"Oh it's poetry. What is it? It sounds rather grand."

"Well, if you can say that perhaps you have got a soul to save. It's Chesterton. One of England's forgotten great men. '*And pleased the pride of a weaker man,*'" I went on. "'*That had yearned for wine or wife; but fame and the flagon, for Mr. Mandragon*'—I mean Mr. Mantovelli—'*obscured the simple life*'."

We could see the lake now and in another minute we were in the village of St. Chamas.

"You look ghastly," he said. "Won't you let me take her? I promise I won't knock her about."

"No. And talking of flagons——"

I pulled up beside a café and opened the door of the car. The heat was almost palpable here. I walked through it and sat down at the nearest table. The wicker awning didn't do much about keeping out the sun.

A man in a dirty apron holding a tray over his head as a shade came out to serve me. "Cognac," I said. "Quickly."

He took one look at me and brought the bottle. It was dark, greasy-looking stuff and the bottle had no label. He pulled the cork and poured out the best part of a glass. It was one of those funnel shaped glasses that you can't very well swig from. Just the same I got the stuff down in two gulps. It was surprisingly good. I pushed the glass towards him. "*Encore*," I said.

He looked up at the sun and looked at me and shook his head. "M'sieu——" he began.

"*Encore*," I said.

He shrugged his shoulders and poured again. I took a

little longer this time. I felt a bit better, too, after the drink had hit me, though I had a pretty good idea that the improvement wouldn't last. I grinned at the man, paid the score and walked back to the car.

Out of St. Chamas we ran down the long slope to the lake. Then the road lies along the shore itself, between the firs and the vine-covered slopes. By the time we got there I knew I'd been a fool. Everything was coming at me at the same time. My shoulder was hurting like hell, my head was roaring and God only knew what was happening inside me.

" '*Mr. Mantovelli, the millionaire, I'm happy to say is dead*'—but he isn't dead, is he?" The yellow road rose suddenly straight up in front of me and then dissolved into a mass of transparent, shimmering lines. I slammed on the brakes and tried my hardest to hold her straight. I knew I wasn't going to succeed, and I had time enough to realize that I had made an uncommon ass of myself. Then a yellow cloud rolled over me and I passed out.

CHAPTER 4

Find the Lady

He had really managed uncommonly well. That was
the first thought which crossed my mind when I
came to. He had got me on to a little shelf in the shelter of
some pines down by the shore of the lake. I was lying on
pine needles with the water about four feet away. A breeze
had got up which was ruffling the surface of the lake, and
some of the killing heat had gone.

He had got a silk scarf, too, out of the car and had
rigged up a sling and put my arm into it. He was sitting on
a rock a few feet from me staring across the lake at the in-
stallations around Martigues. When he heard me move he
stood up and came over to me.

"How are you?" he said.

"I don't know yet. I haven't had time to find out.
Pretty lousy, I should think."

"Will I get you some water from the lake?"

"No. It wouldn't do much good. It's salt. How long
have I been out?"

"Something over an hour. I don't think you were really
out for all that time. You seemed to go to sleep."

"What has happened to the car? Did I smash her up?"

He looked down at me and of all unlikely things I ever
expected to see there I saw something approaching respect
in his glance.

"Hardly at all," he said. "At least that's what I think.

54

She has one wheel in the ditch and the tyre is cut to ribbons and she is down on that side, but that's all."

"I hope so."

"Do you know what we were doing when you went out?"

"No, and I don't think I particularly want to."

"Close on seventy. I don't know how you did it."

"Luck and experience. Let's have a look at her." I stood up. My head went round several times but it came back dead centre and steadied.

"You sure you're all right?" he asked. "Your collar bone hasn't gone, incidentally."

"I know. It's just a ruddy great bang on the shoulder. I'll be O.K. if we take it steady."

There were two long, black brake marks down the right-hand side of the road. At their end was the Bentley. I'd have got away with it if it hadn't been for one of those deep irrigation trenches with which the French have a habit of bordering their roads. The right-hand front wheel had gone into this and skated along it. The sharp stones in the side of the trench had cut the cover in bits and it had wrapped itself round the wheel and the brake drum. The car had stopped down on her front in the ditch. From what I could see there did not appear to be any other damage beyond a few incidental scratches and dents in the coachwork. I mentally blessed the British workmanship which built Bentleys like battleships. But, slight as it was, the damage was beyond our power to repair on the roadside.

"I don't think it's much," I said. "But one of us will have to flag a lift into St. Chamas and get a repair crew with a garage jack. Can you manage that?"

He looked a bit crestfallen. He was learning all sorts of things about himself that day. "It's no good," he said. "I don't know a word of the ruddy language."

"All right. I'll go." I was beginning to feel a good deal better, as a matter of fact. The first, faint heralds of the evening chill were in the air and that helped, too.

At the third attempt we stopped a car. It was a cheerful commercial traveller in a *quatre chevaux*. He drove me into St. Chamas discoursing volubly about his sadness at the damage to *le beau Bentley*.

I hadn't the least doubt that the garage people would be able to put us on the road again. If you give a French mechanic a bent pin he'll tackle a major job on a Nene turbo prop and get away with it, but I also knew enough of the Provençal countryman not to hope to get it done quickly. On both counts I was dead right. The owner of the garage where the commercial traveller dropped me was charming, obviously capable and determined to be helpful, but he had a lot of other jobs to do. These comprised having a long telephone conversation with someone in Aix, drinking a glass of Pastis and offering me one, discussing some involved point of motoring law with an *agent* who happened to stroll by, and having a series of rows with his underlings regarding the timing of an ancient Peugeot.

Finally he pulled a converted Citröen with a crane on it out of the depths of the garage and we set off.

"*Ah, le pauvre Bentley*," he said when he saw the car. "*Ça, c'est beau le Bentley*." He patted the radiator as a man will who fondles a horse. He had been at Le Mans, he said, as a young man and had seen the Bentleys' win in the great years. Ah, M'sieu Bentley, he was a genius.

"Well," I said. "Your M'sieu Buggatti said that M'sieu Bentley had built *le camion le plus vite*."

He was delighted with that old joke and roared with laughter and slapped his thigh, and then, remembering his manners, remarked courteously that it was not, of course, true. I said that M'sieu Bentley had not, in any event, built my car.

Meanwhile one of his men had pulled a big jack out of the Citröen and was at work.

By the time they got the car on the road it was nearly dark and we changed the wheel by the light of an inspection lamp.

"Now, let's get on," Marston said as the last nut went home. "You've a second spare, haven't you?"

"Yes, but just the same I'm afraid that we won't see my aunt tonight."

"Why not?" .

"Her years in the mountains have left her pretty suspicious. She locks the gates at sunset and turns her man-eater, Baskerville, loose in the grounds."

"That means that we've got to stay somewhere for the night."

"Yes, and it might as well be here."

The garage man recommended us to an inn down by the lake. It was a tiny place with pines clustering around it. A little concrete wall was all that separated it from the water. The bedrooms were small and spare and scrubbed and looked out across the lake.

We dined off *salade niçoise* and a huge *assette de fruits de mer* and drank a litre of the local white wine, fresh and sharp and clean on the palate.

We were both hungry. At first neither of us spoke, both, I suppose, busy with our own thoughts. Finally Marston broke the silence.

"Sue?" he said. "Where is she?"

Apparently our thoughts had been much the same. This was just what I had been puzzling over myself.

"In one of three places, I imagine," I said. "Mantovelli's villa at Cap Ferrat, his yacht, which I think is at Villefranche, or at the Château Lubenac, near Apt. My guess is the château. It's lonely and well-guarded at the best of times—just the place for a hostage."

"Hostages don't come to any harm, do they?"

That, too, was what I had been thinking.

"Not without warning. They'll get in touch with us, or with you, rather, and demand a price for her return."

"Price?"

"Yes. Price. I imagine it will be that document you have which they want. They failed to buy it in Ireland. Now they are trying other means. They're going to get it for free. You may not ride as an amateur next season, after all."

"And if I don't hand it over? What can they do? This is the twentieth century."

"Not east of Apt, it isn't. It's more like the thirteenth. Much of that country is all but unexplored. What happens there nobody knows and nobody cares. If they think about it they don't ask questions. A life is not much one way or the other in Haute Provence."

"I see." He devoted his attention to his mullet and silence fell between us again. It was his decision, of course, but I remembered a frightened girl who looked as if fear was foreign to her, and I thought I would stick around until he made it.

With his coffee I ordered him a *fine*. I didn't have one myself. My insides had been taking a pretty good hammering lately and I decided to give them a chance.

He finished it in silence. I thought that I could guess something of what was going on in his mind.

"Another?" I said.

He nodded. "Yes, I think I will."

I called Madame and she set a fresh glass in front of him.

"What is it like?" I asked.

"Not bad. I don't know much about these things. They all taste pretty well the same to me. Look—there is no alternative, is there?"

"If there is I can't see it."

"You think that if I do give them what they want they'll let her go?"

"I'm sure of it. She's only an embarrassment."

"Well, then, I suppose that's it. You've always had money, haven't you, Herald? You've never known what it is like to want to do something more than anything else in the world and then not be able to do it."

"You might be surprised," I said, but I don't think he heard me.

"I was five years a learner in a racing stable—Leatherby's," he went on. "I left school early to go into it. It was bloody tough. Old Chris Leatherby was one of the hard and rough school of trainers. I learnt how to do a couple of horses and how to hold my own in a race and in the yard. I didn't learn much else. That's why I don't know anything about what to drink or how to talk French or that stuff you were quoting. Who did you say he was that wrote it, by the way?"

"Chesterton. Nobody reads him now, but between the wars he and Belloc and Flecker and Brooke, they were the poets of youth. Young men went around drunk on their rhythms and wrote public school novels for the pleasure of quoting them. A cabinet minister wrote a novel about Rossall, a leader writer wrote one about Loretto, John Heygate wrote *Decent Fellows*. No one knows how many more were written and about what schools, but one and all their heroes, who were the angry young men of those days, recited chunks of Heraclitus or the War Song of The Saracens or Lepanto. So did we all, come to think of it. For that matter I, too, in my time have dreamt of taking the Golden Road to Samarkand and watching the high peaks hoar along the Aragon. But it's all as dated now as a blown Bentley and the people who drove one. And I'm a maudlin middle-aged man. I've had a heavy day. I'm going to turn in. Good night."

I undressed quickly; when I crossed to the window to draw the curtains he was standing below me on the terrace, smoking a cigarette, its red tip glowing in the darkness. All was quite still and there was the scent of thyme in the air. I didn't disturb his thoughts. Although he didn't know it I had a pretty good idea of what they were.

Turning back the sheets I got into the wide, comfortable bed which took up nearly half the room. Tomorrow or the next day it would all be over. He had made his decision. She would be set free and I would go on to the Coast without them, free, too, of their youth and the disturbance they had wrought in me. For I knew that I badly wanted to see her again and to go on seeing her. Yet there was nothing for her in a battered wreck like me. I was far better out of the way for good and all.

It was their youth, I supposed, which had caused the old rhymes to ring once more in my brain, which had set me reeling off half-forgotten poems and talking of wholly forgotten novels. I closed my eyes and stretched my aching limbs. My arm was much easier. Well, it had been an interesting interlude. *We are they who come faster than fate: we are they who ride early or late: we storm at your*

ivory gate. . . . They told me, Heraclitus, they told me you were
dead. . . . The fresh tang of the great salt lake came through
the open window mingled with the sweet smell of the
pines and of the thyme on the hillsides. *How often you and*
I had tired the sun with talking and sent him down the sky. . . .
And he smiles, but not as sultans smile and settles back the blade
(But Don John of Austria rides home from the Crusade). . . .
Evening on the olden, the golden sea of Wales, when the first star
shivers and the last wave pales. . . .

I closed my eyes. I was asleep in five minutes.

Next morning I awoke with a clear head and a clean
mouth. I had had ten hours' sleep without the assistance of
barbiturates or alcohol, and except for an ache in my
shoulder and some of my muscles I felt better than I had
done for weeks.

We were up early and we should have been early away.

But we found one of the back tyres punctured and this
took time to repair. Then, just beyond the Acqueduct, in
that bit of country which is not unlike Surrey with its
maze of little roads and hedgerows, I took a wrong turning
and we found ourselves on the outskirts of Aix. This
meant retracing our steps and then, like a fool, I proceeded
to get thoroughly lost. So that it was after midday when
we went up the concrete drive of Mas Melanie, my aunt's
villa.

An opulent-looking black and yellow Rolls was drawn
up by the front door, but my aunt was pruning roses at the
side of the house. Baskerville was lying at her side. He got
to his feet and came slowly towards us, ugly and menacing,
his hackles up, his head between his shoulder blades, his
upper lip drawn back in a snarl. Baskerville was your real
man-eater; he never bothered with empty barking; he
looked at you and then came in like lightning. As a result

of intervention from the *gendarmerie* he was now muzzled in the daytime, but just the same I eyed him with respect and I walked round him at a respectable distance as I approached my aunt. He followed me a pace behind, breathing down the backs of my legs. Baskerville and I had never been soul-mates and I was very conscious that muzzles, especially when put on by my Aunt Dorothy, often afforded very little protection to the public.

I halted a full five yards away from her. "Aunt Dorothy," I said. "Call off your keeper, will you? He makes me nervous."

My aunt lowered the pruning knife and looked up. "Ah, dear Simon," she said. "It is nice to see you. Come here, Basky. Come here, boy."

The dog obeyed her and lay down at her side.

"Isn't he sweet?" she said, looking at him fondly.

As if daring me to say something Baskerville's little yellow eyes stared at me belligerently. He was, I noticed, just beginning to run to fat. He looked like a vicious tramp who has hung up his hat in a comfortable home, is on to a good thing and knows it.

My aunt was wearing—if you can believe it—a tweed skirt and one of those high-collared blue and white striped blouses so popular in the eighteen nineties. It was held at the neck by a cameo brooch, and on her head was a tweed cap. She was a handsome woman and she looked remarkably well in this outfit if a trifle out of place, for the heat was such that the thermometer was practically on the boil.

Marston had followed me and I introduced him. "Aunt Dorothy," I said. "Did you get a letter from me this morning?"

"Yes, indeed, Simon. Most interesting it was, too.

What *is* in that envelope, dear? You know, often I don't open my post for weeks. But just today I did happen to. Wasn't it lucky?"

"Yes, Aunt Dorothy. I wonder, perhaps, if you would mind giving it back to me now." I should have known better than to entrust something of value to her, I told myself. I had not been registering very well that night and, anyway, a long separation had softened my recollection of her vagueness and eccentricity. A faint foreboding was beginning to creep into my mind.

"Who was that man in that book who said that if you have something precious to keep—it was dear Mr. Chute, I think, or perhaps it was that nice woman who writes about Barsetshire, or Miss Christie, was it?"

"Or Enid Blyton?" I suggested, my head whirling.

My aunt laughed, a deep throaty chuckle, and gave me a sharp look. She had a way of surprising you sometimes. "You mustn't make fun of me, Simon," she said. "What was it now, we were talking about? Oh, mercy me, I black forgot. We have a visitor. Come along in."

Without waiting for an answer she dropped the pruning knife into the basket at her feet and led the way into the house through an open french window. There was nothing to do but follow and this we did.

He looked immense in the little room full of the spindly bric-à-brac of an earlier generation. He was standing in front of the fireplace, all six foot four of him, in that attitude of studied drama affected by certain officers in the heavy cavalry. He brought his own menace with him, too.

Stuart Jason was my aunt's visitor.

"Marston I know," he said in his imperious way as my aunt introduced us. "It was in the hope of meeting him that I made so bold as to take up your time and your house." He bowed slightly towards my aunt, and smiled with studied charm. He had, I was pleased to notice, a strip of sticking plaster along the side of his jaw. "Your nephew, however——"

"We have not formally met," I said, looking at the sticking-plaster.

"If you would be so kind as to allow me five minutes with these gentlemen," Jason said to my aunt, "I have something of importance to discuss with them. We could have a room, perhaps?"

"You must stay here," my aunt said. "I know. I shall get you a glass of port wine and a biscuit." She bustled out. Baskerville gave us all a glance of contempt and dislike from his little yellow eyes and followed her.

"Now, a word with you, Marston," Jason said immediately the door closed.

"Yes."

"If you value your sister's life you will hand that formula over to me."

"What are you going to give me for it?"

"Your sister's safety."

Marston hesitated. He was out of his depth. He glanced at me.

Ever since I had spoken to my aunt I had had the uneasy feeling that she had done something clever with the envelope. Heaven alone knew what it was. One thing was certain, however, and that was that she must not be involved in this. At the moment it was clear that I must play for time until I could talk to her again.

"What guarantee have we got that you will keep your side of the bargain?" I asked him.

"I am not addressing any remarks to you," he replied.

"I shall have something to settle with you later. Meanwhile confine yourself to your own concerns."

"Christ! Who the hell do you think you are? You are not talking to a lot of scared subalterns now, Jason. I happen to have been given that envelope and I've put it somewhere safe."

He ignored me and looked steadily at Marston.

"I shall be in the Café des Sports at Apt at noon tomorrow," he said. "It is in the Place de la Bouquerie. Your sister will be with me. You, too, will be there—*alone*. We will make the exchange. Is that clear?"

Marston nodded.

Then, for the first time, Jason turned to look directly at me. For an instant something jumped and flamed in his eyes. It was terrifying in the sudden revelation of the urge to hurt and destroy he carried around with him. It was like a lamp of evil suddenly switched on.

"Keep away from Apt tomorrow, Herald," he said. "That is a warning. I'll just add that it will give me great pleasure if you disregard it."

"I suppose Mantovelli paid your racing debts," I said to him. "Is that why you do his dirty work for him or is it because you like it?"

"You will live—if you do live—to regret saying that." There was such naked menace in his voice that I thought I might, too.

He turned to Marston. "You have just under twenty-four hours to make up your mind," he said. He stood quite still for a moment without speaking, his presence commanding the little room. Then he smiled. It was a sudden death's head grin; there was no humour in it at all. He looked for a moment at me. Then he walked past us to the door and shut it quietly behind him. The Rolls purred off down the drive. My knees felt suddenly and stupidly weak. He had frightened me and I hated him for it.

"Arrogant swine," I said. "He only needs a Von in front of his name to be a Hun."

"He is one. Didn't you know? His grandfather commanded a regiment of the Prussian Guard."

"Good Lord——"

At that moment my aunt came back into the room. She had four glasses of rich, red, ruby port on a salver. They were wine-glasses and big ones, the sort of things you swill *vin ordinaire* out of. I looked at the great heavy draught she handed me and then at the sun outside. I thought of heat-stroke and several other things. Not that I couldn't have done with a drink, and a strong one, too, just at that moment. "Aunt Dorothy," I said. "Port—it's a little heavy for me at this time of day. You wouldn't have any *Pastis* perhaps?"

"No, dear, what is that? Has our visitor gone? I didn't at all take to him, did you? Oh, dear, now I've said the wrong thing. Is he a great friend of yours, Mr. Marston?"

"Aunt Dorothy," I said. "What did you do with that envelope?"

She sat down in a tall wooden chair and folded her hands in her lap. "Yes, Simon. We were talking about that before, weren't we? Well, you see, Simon, it's so difficult for a woman and a foreigner living alone, even with dear, dear Baskerville to look after me. One does get so suspicious. Oh, I do hope I haven't done something dreadful——"

"If you would just tell us what you have done, Aunt Dorothy?"

"Well, yesterday there was a telephone call. A most

brusque-mannered man. He was looking for you, Simon, or rather he was looking for your friend, Mr. Marston. He was not at all nice. Then, this morning, this Colonel Jason called. He was looking for Mr. Marston, too. I confess I didn't take to him at all. Oh, I've said that before, haven't I? We must love our fellow-men, of course, but must we *like* them? I often wonder——"

She was off at a tangent again.

"Yes, Aunt Dorothy," I said firmly. "The letter, remember."

"Yes, the letter. I really thought—oh, dear, it does seem silly, perhaps, now. But you know, Simon, it was all so *odd*. That telephone call and then that *horrible* Colonel Jason. I really thought I had better send it somewhere safe. Do you know what I did?"

"No, Aunt Dorothy, I don't. And without wanting to fuss or bother you, I've been waiting three quarters of an hour to find out."

"Well, when the postman came I read the letter. Something told me it was to do with that horrible man waiting inside. Oh, my goodness, I do hope——"

"Aunt Dorothy!"

"I there and then sat down and sent it off to your wife in Ireland to keep it safely for you."

CHAPTER 5

Excursions Autour d'Apt

Behind me, from Roddy Marston, there was the sound of something like a groan.

"I do hope I did right, dear Simon," my aunt said.

"It was most ingenious of you, Aunt Dorothy. Miss Sayers would have been proud of you, Miss Christie would pat you on the back," I said, gravely. I rather felt like having hysterics.

"Thank you, dear. Do you know I think I'll just go and finish the roses."

"What now?" Marston asked.

"Damned if I know. Let me think for a moment. You've made up your mind to hand this thing over?"

"What else can I do?"

"Well, the midday plane from Nice is out. We haven't a hope of making it."

"No." It all seemed beyond him. He had no suggestions to offer. "I wonder—Maurice Kenway is on the Coast with his Apache. He might just get us there and back in time. I'll ring Cannes airfield. It's a long shot but we might catch him."

The call came through surprisingly quickly. No, they said, M'sieu Kenway had left that morning. It was not a local flight. One moment, please, while they looked up the flight plan. M'sieu Kenway had left for Le Touquet and Croydon.

"That's that," I said, putting down the receiver.

"I'll just have to go there and when Jason comes tell him what has happened."

"He won't even begin to believe you. And he certainly won't believe me." I had been thinking while I waited for the phone call. I was in this now, up to the neck. In fact I was responsible for getting Marston and his sister into this damnably dangerous predicament. It was up to me to get them out of it—if I could. "There is one other possibility," I said. "We'll have to rescue her before noon tomorrow."

"How the hell can we do that? We don't even know where she is."

"We have a damn good idea. At least I have. I'll lay all Lombard Street to a china orange that she is in the Château Lubenac. Jason's choice of Apt for a rendezvous confirms it. Wait a moment while I get my maps." I went out to the car and opened the glove compartment. Inside was a bundle of Michelin maps held together with a rubber band. Back in the room I snapped off the band and spread sheet 84 on the table. Inside the cover I found the other thing I was looking for. I examined it closely and then put it down on the opened map. It was the card which Mantovelli's secretary had sent me describing the route to the chateau. "*Excursions autour d'Apt*," I said. "We're going to take one that is not in the Michelin guide. That is if you are game. It might be even more dangerous than riding in a novice chase at Newbury."

"Of course I am if it is going to help Sue. And there is no need to be bloody about it."

"Very well. It shouldn't take us long to get there." I studied the map, working out our route. "An hour at the most if we press on."

"What then?"

"Come over here a second and look at this map." I put my finger on the tangle of wooded hills almost immediately south-east of Apt. "The château is here or hereabouts. We'll have to find it first, of course, and it may not be quite as simple as it looks. We'll be coming at it from exactly the opposite direction from the arrows on the sketch. And we can't exactly drive up to the door and ask the butler where the dungeons are. Still, we'll have plenty of daylight. We should manage it."

"What are you going to do when you get there?"

"Break into the château and take her away. It's as easy as that."

"I suppose you know what you are doing."

"I haven't the least idea. But this is one of the occasions when one just has to go on by guess and by God."

He looked at me again. "I wish——" he started to say, then he closed his mouth and bit the sentence off unfinished.

"I know what you wish," I said. "You wish you had someone of your own sort to lead you. Well you've got me and you'll have to put up with me. Without me you couldn't even get yourself into Aix, let alone to Apt. One more thing—however much you dislike it, for the next twenty-four hours I am in charge. You'll do as I say. Understand?"

The surly look of the spoilt child came on to his face again and he hesitated. Then he appeared to recognize the inevitable. "All right," he said. "Until we get my sister out. Then I'm on my own."

"It's a deal."

"Wait a second—that formula, envelope, I mean. Your wife has it now. It is mine. Write her a letter telling her to hand it over to me when I call for it."

"What is the formula for?"

"I'm not going to tell you."

"Is it anything to do with a Service secret?"

"No. Nothing. It's a private matter."

"Do you swear that?"

"Yes."

There was nothing much else I could do but believe him.

"All right, I'll give you that letter." I went over and wrote a few lines to Mildred on Aunt Dorothy's writing paper. "This may not do you much good," I said to him as I gave it to him. "Mildred and I have bust up. Still, you can try."

We took our leave of my aunt and refused her pressing invitation to luncheon.

"Oh, dear," she said. "People do seem to drop in so unexpectedly these days. I hope I did right about that letter, Simon."

"You did splendidly, Aunt Dorothy," I said. "I'll send you the new Agatha Christie for Christmas."

Back in the car I leant down and made sure that the dampers were tight. Then I let in the clutch.

I looked at my watch. It was two o'clock. We should want to make what time we could. He realized this too.

"Now, I suppose we'll really see how Daddy does it," he said.

"Daddy's going to try," I answered.

I cut out Aix altogether and struck north. In a few minutes we had crossed the main highway and were on our way to the Durance and Cadenet.

I was trying all right. My changes were going in like the proverbial hot knife through butter. I wasn't taking risks; I was concentrating like hell and I was leaving the miles piled up behind me in the heat.

The ordinary standard Mark VI steel Bentley has a maximum of about ninety. But mine was not quite the standard model. I had had the compression raised and done certain other minor modifications, and wear had increased the capacity. As a consequence my maximum was somewhere nearer one hundred and ten, and, if you knew how to use the gears, she took precious little time to get there.

As we went I thought of the old Bentley. *Le camion le plus vite*. Like most good epigrams M. Buggatti's was clever, cutting and about a quarter true. "Great, green battle-cruisers," someone else had called them. But, criticize them how you will, those old Bentleys had an ability to inspire affection no other car ever had or will have, and although they had ceased production by the time I grew up the Bentley was still, in the thirties, the car *par excellence* for a young man to own. Much of my youth was bound up with them and the days we thundered laughing up the London road. Those enormous, slightly forward looking radiators with the proud winged B on them seemed to yearn for speed. And, as I remembered, we saw to it that they got it. Twelve years is a short time for a motor-car to make itself immortal yet that span covered the life of the first Bentley. It took W. O. Bentley only twelve years to write his name in motor-racing history and to create a legend. It was the magic and memory of the winged B which had really made me buy the car I was sitting in now.

But the upper reaches of speed are no time or place for day-dreaming. On the long straight before Rognes the road was clear. I put my foot down and felt the revs build up. The needle on the central speedometer went climbing across the dial. It reached three figures and stayed there. "The whole ton" they called it nowadays, I reflected.

Even at that speed the big engine in front of me was

72

only whispering. She sat like a rock on the road. Our progress was silent save for the thresh of the tyres.

Beside me I felt rather than saw him move a little in his seat, and I knew that movement. I had seen it before in cars and aeroplanes. He passed a hand over his hair. I could read the signs; he wasn't liking it. It was more than probable he hadn't been as fast as this before. I smiled to myself. Daddy could show him something after all.

Then I saw the *camions*.

There were two of them, sand lorries, fully loaded, bucketing along line astern. Some of their load was weeping on to the road as they went. They were going our way.

There was room enough to take them, or I thought there was. I had my revs now and I didn't want to lose them. I aimed for the gap and, as happens on these occasions, it narrowed as we neared it.

I was in position to pass then the third *camion* came into it. The roof of his cab showed suddenly above a slope of ground on the left. He was in a field making for the road. The driver was leaning out, looking behind him and shouting to a chum. It appeared likely that the three of us would arrive at the same point at the same moment. And I was doing one hundred and five miles an hour.

The course, speed and distance of all of us went through my eyes and into my brain in the way they will. The answer came out that we should have about five yards to spare. Provided, of course, that the driver of the third lorry did not catch sight of us and panic. It would be just too bad if he hit the accelerator instead of the brake. He never turned around. His conversation held him deaf to the noise of our approach. Which was just as well for it was going to be closer than I thought. The clearance was nearer nothing than five yards.

I felt an all but overmastering desire to lift my foot and knew that we should die if I did so. There was nothing for it but to hold to our course and hope. The great towering radiator of the *camion* was suddenly right over us, shutting out the sun. There was a rock and a slam. Then we were through.

A long, hissing exhalation of breath came from the boy beside me.

"Daddy does that every day, usually before breakfast," I said.

"You needn't think you're frightening me."

"Congratulations. I've just terrified myself."

As we ran into Pertuis I said to him, "We'll stop here and buy something to eat and drink. I'm beginning to regret Aunt Dorothy's lunch."

Parking the car beside a bus in the Place I went in search of an *alimentation*. There I bought a couple of tins of the local *pâté*, toasted *bisquits*, butter and cheese and peaches. Across the road I got a litre of red wine and a loaf of the incomparable crisp French bread. Then I went back to the car.

Storm clouds were piling up away to the west when we neared Lourmarin. But it was still desperately hot, not with the oppressive heat of an approaching storm but with the clear, scorching heat of Provence. Beyond Lourmarin we dived into the dark cleft in the hills which is the gateway to the Luberon Mountains. For a short time as we commenced the long haul up the pass we were in the shade of the hills.

Where the road divides and the country breaks up into a multitude of little valleys I stopped the car and took out Mantovelli's sketch.

A wilderness of woods and waste and scrub surrounded

us. Almond trees and stunted oaks grew in profusion all over the sides of the valleys. Behind was the main mass of the Luberons. We had made good time; even with the stop in Pertuis we had covered fifty miles of mainly mountain road in well under the hour.

"Now," I said, looking at my watch. "We have a good three hours of daylight to find the place, if that damned *orage* over there doesn't come up and catch us in the meantime. Give me the map, will you?"

He handed it to me. I unfolded it and spread it against the steering wheel. "Do you see that minor road?" I said putting my finger on it. "That is where I think the château is. Somewhere between that road and the mountains."

"How are you going to get into it?"

"I don't know yet. We've got to find it first. We also have to hide the car."

About a mile down the road I turned the Bentley off on to a track leading into the scrub. There was no difficulty at all about finding a place to leave her. I simply backed her into a space between the trees and there she was hidden. It was very still; we had met no one since we had left Lourmarin twelve kilometres away. We were quite alone in the sun and the heat. We might as well have been on Mars.

"Food before battle," I said, taking the provisions out of the back of the car.

We got what shelter we could from the sun under the stunted trees. I gave him a glass of wine whilst I opened the *pâté*. Then I handed him the tin.

"What is this?" he asked, looking at it suspiciously.

"It's the local *pâté* and costs about two shillings a go. It tastes rather better than the *foie gras* for which you pay half a guinea a postage stamp in England. Try it."

75

He spread some on to the *bisquit*, and, after a moment, bit a piece off. He munched and swallowed. Then he reached out and cut himself another, larger, portion. When he had finished this his look of suspicion disappeared. "It *is* good," he said. "Where did you find out all these things, Herald? And where did you learn to speak French?"

"Slightly caddish attributes, aren't they? The same as driving fast motor-cars."

"I never said that."

"No, but I can tell what is going on in your mind. Have some wine. I'm sorry it's not a whisky and soda."

He held out his glass and I filled it. "Why are you always trying to ride me?" he asked, glowering.

I looked down at my own glass. "I'm not riding you," I said. "I don't know. Perhaps I am. Perhaps it's because I think you have a soul to save, somewhere. Let's get on now." There was a pair of binoculars in the back of the car. I took these out and locked her up. Then we walked down the track the way we had come.

"I picked this particular track for a purpose," I said. "It's in case we get separated. There are thousands of them running off the roads hereabouts and they all look the same. But here is something which will tell you that this is the one you want." I pointed to an old, half-buried kilometre stone set in the side of the road. "Got it?"

"O.K."

I had a look at the sun and another look at the storm clouds piling up somewhere east of Avignon, and then we started out across the scrub.

It was tough going in the heat. The ground was rough underfoot. The sun sat up behind us like a burnished half-penny piece. One could almost see the rays of heat sparking off from it. Except for the black mass in the distance there was not a cloud in the sky. Before we had covered a quarter of a mile we were both of us pouring sweat and beginning to wilt.

The trouble was, of course, that from the direction we were approaching I could not pin-point the château. And since each ridge might hide it we had to go down on our stomachs at every skyline to make sure of what was beyond.

Over the first two there was nothing but valleys filled with trees and waste and scrub. We crossed these, making our way as best we could along the winding tracks. The branches tore at our clothes and the heat beat up from the hard, baked earth. As best I could I set course south and east. We crossed another ridge and it was clear that we were now backing up towards the main mass of the Luberon Mountains. I was rapidly realizing that the whole business was much more hit and miss than I had anticipated. Unless we were lucky it was quite possible that we might not find the château at all before dark. One can never really size up a country from a small-scale map and the ground was proving even more broken than I had guessed.

The next ridge we came to was a false crest.

"I suppose this place does exist?" Marston sat down and mopped his face with his handkerchief. "Or have you just made a balls of your map-reading?"

"It's here all right—somewhere. Have you had enough? Will I go on and send Nanny back for you?"

"No, damn you." He stood up again.

The rise in front of us was very steep. The last fifty feet or so we were climbing, pulling ourselves up by trees and finding footholds in the rocks.

On a ledge ten feet from the top we stopped for a breather. To our left a dry watercourse rose steeply to the crest.

"Wait for me here," I said. "I'll go to the top alone."

I made my way up the bed of the watercourse, climbing over the rocks and loose stones. A thin screen of bushes ran along the skyline. I lay beneath them for a few moments, my head in the rough foliage at their roots, getting my breath. Then I stretched out my hand and, very gently, made myself a gap through which I could see.

Down below me was one of those lush green valleys you come on sometimes so unaccountably in those mountains. It was in the shape of a bowl and was formed by two spurs running out from the main chain of hills. From where I lay to its far side was probably about half a mile. In its centre, lying in the full glare of the sun, with a drive of tall cypresses leading away from it, was Mantovelli's château.

It was a great, square-built, cream-coloured house, four storeys high. At each corner was a tower topped with a gnome's hat roof of red tiles. The main roof was low-pitched and jutted over the top row of windows giving the house a sort of permanent frown. At first floor level a pillared and balustraded loggia ran the length of the house.

I reached down and took the binoculars out of their case. A glance at the sun told me I was in no danger of giving myself away by catching its reflection on the glasses. I put them to my eyes and focused them on the house.

There was no movement anywhere. Inside the cool depths of the loggia I could see lounging chairs and tables, but no one sat there. The shutters were across all the windows which did not surprise me. Down in that bowl in the hills with the sun on it it must have been like the inside of a furnace. Still, the old millionaire's blood was thin and his skin like leather and perhaps that was what he wanted.

Between where I lay and the house was a park and then there were lawns cropped and cut and a big stone fountain. Huge chestnut trees grew in the park and I could just see one side of a formal garden. Behind rose the main pile of the Luberons scored with long streaks of bare rock like scars on flesh.

As I watched, a man came into view from between the cypresses of the avenue. He walked slowly down the side of the house in front of me. Something about him seemed familar and I turned the glasses on to him. It was the same huge brute who had attacked us in Arles. He turned round the far corner of the house and disappeared. I can't say the sight of him cheered me up. Another encounter might turn out differently.

I put the glasses back in their case. Below me Marston was waiting and I slid down the watercourse to him.

"We've arrived," I said briefly. "The château is over that ridge. So, if it is of any interest to you, is that man-mountain you toppled down the steps in Arles. I hope you are in good fighting form. He's a bit over my weight."

"I expect I can manage him. What is the next move?"

"I want to try to find out where Sue is in the château. Is there any noise you could make which she would recognize? Anything that would make her come to a window or show a signal?"

"I could holloa."

"That'd be a fat lot of good. Jason's in there, remember. Stupid as I am sure he is, he still isn't likely to expect the Heytrop Hounds to come pouring across his park. Try again."

He thought for a few moments. "When we were kids we used to yodel to each other," he said.

"That is a bit better. At least it isn't a certainty that he'll know we're here. Now, look, directly above us one side of the château faces where we are. I want you to work around under cover until you can command another. That way we can watch all the windows of two sides. Ten minutes ought to be enough to get you into position. When you are there go into your act with the yodel. Just once, we can't risk any more. Wait another ten minutes watching the house. Then come back here. If neither of us has seen her we'll have to try the other sides. Get it?"

"Yes."

"All right. We'll synchronize our watches. And for heaven's sweet sake keep under cover and don't do anything stupid. These aren't the heights of Balaclava, in case you've forgotten."

He put his watch right, gave me a look into which all his dislike of the past few days was compressed, and set off.

I climbed up the watercourse again. With the glasses I searched every inch of the house looking for a possible way in. The loggia was the obvious place for an approach but the trouble was how to reach it. We had no ropes and even if we had it was too high from the ground unless we had assistance from inside. A riot of purple bougainvilleas climbed over the pillars and the balustrade and cascaded to the ground. To the left, where the tower joined the house, there was a great magnolia tree, flat against the wall. I looked at it more closely and an idea began to be born in my mind. It reached from the top of the loggia to the ground. If one could climb it, and some magnolias are tough and strong and well able to take the weight of a man, one could surely swing across the gap to the balustrade of the loggia. Moreover, it was a right-handed gap so the strain would not come on my bad arm. I was so intent on this that I had forgotten the minutes ticking by. Suddenly I was jerked back to more immediate concerns, for a yodel rang out, surprisingly clear and true across the still air. It was some four hundred miles and two centuries out of place. I hoped Jason was still sleeping off his lunch.

I swept the side of the house with the glasses. A minute passed and another. Nothing moved. The house basked in the sun, the shutters were locked and motionless. I brought the glasses back to the loggia and ran them along it. There also nothing stirred.

Then, suddenly, I caught my breath. In the very centre of the loggia, at the back was a sudden flash of white. A curtain had been drawn or a door had been opened. Someone stood there in the depths. I pressed the glasses to my eyes and tried to penetrate the gloom. Then I caught my breath again. A girl in a white skirt walked slowly to the balustrade, shading her eyes against the sun. She waved a hand across her face. It might have been a gesture to brush something away, but it was held a second longer than the normal gesture. She put her hands on the balustrade and leant there for a few moments, gazing at the hills, looking at a point somewhere close to where the yodel had come from. Then she turned and walked back out of sight. It was Sue Marston.

Five minutes later he joined me on the ledge. "She is there all right," I said. "Come up top again and I'll show you the layout and where we are going."

Before I gave the glasses to him I had another look at the magnolia. Nothing is ever as easy as one hopes and there was in fact quite a considerable gap between the tree and the balustrade. But it was the only way in, and I thought we should be able to manage it. I handed him the glasses.

"She is somewhere behind the centre portion of that loggia," I said. "When you have located that take a look at the magnolia on the left-hand tower."

"Is that your way in?" he said after a few minutes.

"I hope so. Any questions?"

"It'll be a bit of a stretch. What about your arm?"

"It's my good arm. I'll have to chance it. Now let's memorize the ground between here and the house."

From the top of the ridge where we lay the ground was broken and fell steeply for some hundreds of yards to where the parkland began. The formal garden was on the right, the avenue of cypresses to the left. The only cover on the approach was afforded by one of the chestnuts and the fountain, a stone bowl in which stood a figurine of a little boy with an urn.

"Two jumps," I said. "The tree and the fountain, and then we're in, we hope."

As I spoke a red car hurtled down between the cypresses and disappeared round the far corner of the house.

"That's the Ferrari," I said. "Perhaps Jason was out. If so we're in luck, and he never heard you yodel. We'd better go in about three o'clock, and hope they are all asleep. These nights are pretty clear. We should be able to see our way. We'll just have to chance the guards."

"What about that?" He nodded at the storm. It was piling up behind us bigger and blacker than ever.

"Maybe it will miss us. You never know where they go in these hills. We've got some time to kill, so four hours on and four hours off. You are younger than I am. First stint to you."

I improvised shelter under some trees on the ledge, kicked myself into what comfort I could and shut my eyes. I had just time to think that at least he was keeping pretty well to his part of the bargain about taking orders but that there would probably be some trouble about this later on, and then that something must be happening to me for here I was slipping into sleep in the afternoon without benefit of barbiturates or alcohol. Then, believe it or not, I was asleep.

When we climbed over the crest to go down to the château, the storm was massing behind us and the air was thick and heavy. "Make for the tree," I said, and we went on quickly and in silence.

All was still as we crouched in the deep shade of the big chestnut. Not the faintest breeze sighed through the leaves. The great house brooded beside us; the air was like a blanket about us. We left the tree and crossed the cropped grass towards the fountain. Five yards from it I caught his shoulder and pushed him to the ground.

A man had turned the corner of the house by the magnolia. He stopped for a moment under the loggia where Sue had been that afternoon, glanced up at it and moved on. A moment later he was out of sight beyond the far turret. He had a machine-pistol cradled in his arm.

"Quick," I said. "He's on a beat. Up the magnolia and wait for me on the loggia."

He sprinted across and went up hand over fist. When I saw him over the balustrade I left the shelter of the fountain.

It had looked easy enough when he did it. I had forgotten the twenty or so years between us. It was harder going than I had thought. I had to stop and grope for hand-holds and I wasn't as quick as I once should have been in finding them. When I was up where the stretch across to the balustrade came, I was out of breath and panting. I was worried about the guard, too. If he had only to go round the house he must be back any moment now. Stuck up here like a fly on a fly-paper I was a sitting shot. And from what I knew of the outfit I didn't imagine he would stop to ask questions.

I tried to get my feet right for the stretch. My heart was jumping and banging against my ribs from the effort of the climb and I cursed it and my own weakness. A piece of creeper broke away beneath me and fell flaking on to the flags below. Involuntarily I looked down. Hard and cold in the dawn light they waited for me to spill myself on to them. My mouth went dry and the back of my knees began to tremble.

There was nothing for it; I must go now or not at all. My weight and my handholds were all wrong, but if I waited I should either confess myself a coward and afraid to face it or fall.

Setting my teeth I launched myself across the gap. I missed my grip and the pull came on my left arm. An excruciating pain shot through it up to the shoulder. My right hand clawed again for a hold on the balustrade—and found it. I was across the gap but my left arm was useless. I was straddled in mid-air and what grip I had was going. The flags gleamed palely below and I thought I heard the tread of the guard.

A hand came out from the shadows, caught me under the armpit and lifted me. I got my foot on to the balustrade, kicked myself over and came down on all fours on the floor.

The footsteps of the guard went past below.

I got up, dusted myself off and looked at the boy standing beside me.

"Thanks," I said when I had got my breath back.

I had been right in my guess. A curtain hung across an archway at the back of the loggia. We parted it and found ourselves in a big, airy, panelled room with a floor of red tiles and long windows opening on to the loggia.

In a fourposter bed facing us she was fast asleep. Her arm, bare and brown and shapely, lay outside the covers. I put my hand on it and pressed gently. "Sue," I said softly "Sue, we're here."

She came awake as the young come awake, wide-open and fresh on the instant.

"Get up and dress—quickly," I said. "We haven't much time."

For I had miscalculated. It had all taken longer than I had thought. The night was lifting every minute.

"I can't."

"Why not? Don't be missish, there isn't time for it. We won't look."

"They take all my clothes away every night! I've nothing on!"

I turned to him. "Take your trousers off," I said.

"What! !"

"You heard me. She has to wear something. You'll look very well in your B.V.D.'s." I was pulling my shirt off as I spoke. I threw it on to the bed. "Come on," I said to her. "We'll turn our backs. Let us know when you are ready. And by all that's merciful get a move on."

We heard the rustle of bedclothes as we turned away and the soft whisper of her body as she slid from the bed. In a few moments she told us she was dressed. She came towards us pushing her hair back from her eyes. She looked tousled and defenceless and damnably attractive.

"Can you get her across the gap and down the magnolia?" I asked him.

"Yes, if I go first and catch her."

"Off you go then. Wait—let the guard go by first. There he is now." The sound of his steps on the flags came quite clearly up to us. They died away round the corner of the house. "Once you are down make for the car," I said.

"What about you?"

"I'll manage on my own. Get cracking. You haven't all that time."

They went along the loggia and I turned back to the bedroom. I knew I couldn't face the descent of the magnolia. My arm would not get me across the gap, and I doubted if my nerve would stand it, either. I ripped the sheets off the bed and started knotting them together. There wasn't an awful lot in the way of bedclothes for she had been sleeping light but I had to chance that. I hoped they would reach the ground or near enough to it to give me a chance to jump.

I had to wait, too, until the guard had gone past once more. Then I tied one end of the sheets to the balustrade, threw the other over and went after it.

I was nearly down when I realized that the guard was coming back. Something about their flight must have attracted his attention for when he came into my view he was looking out over the park. Above him, on the wall, I was in the shade of the house and for the moment he had not seen me. But it was only a matter of seconds before he did. There was just one thing for me to do. There was just one chance, too. I had to do it right or not at all. I got my foot against one of the shutters, let my hands slip down the sheets and bunched myself into a ball with all my muscles ready.

He came on slowly, some way out from me. It would not be a direct drop. About ten feet from me he stopped and again turned to peer across the park. I took a deep breath. Then I kicked myself through the air towards him. I fell on top of him like a sack falling out of a hoist. He crumpled and we went down together in a heap on to the flags. I heard the hollow bang of his head hitting and felt him go limp underneath me. The machine-pistol went skating and clattering out of his hands. I picked myself up, bent down to grab the gun, and ran. As I went all hell broke loose behind me.

I hadn't covered more than fifty yards when I saw the two of them coming back towards me. "Get on, you young fools," I said, "You should be at the car by now."

Together we ran across the grass. A shot flayed over our heads. I turned round, pulled back the cocking handle of the tommy-gun and let go a burst into the blue. "That may discourage them from getting too close," I said.

We ran on. We were far from our point of approach. Dawn was coming up fast but so were the storm clouds. We reached the foothills and started up the rougher, steeper going. The sounds of pursuit had stopped for a moment. Maybe my burst had temporarily halted them.

We went on climbing and very shortly I knew I was cooked. Too many pink gins and too little exercise had finished me for running for my life. My leg had always put a bit of a period to this sort of activity but I could have managed that I think. It was my lack of condition which was stopping me. My breath was coming in great gasps and there was a racking pain in my chest. I began to fall behind.

They stopped and he came back to me. "Go on," I said. "I'm done."

"If you can't keep up we'll have to stay with you."

"I've got the gun. I'll be all right."

"Don't be a fool. We can't leave you now."

"I'm ordering you to go on with Sue. I thought I was in command here."

"Until we got her out you were. I'm not taking orders any longer."

At that moment the storm broke. The rain came down all about us in solid drenching sheets. There was a growl of thunder, a blinding flash and then, on top of it, a ringing crash right over our heads.

We stood facing each other like two fools. "Are you coming on?" he shouted over the din of the storm.

"No." I *was* done. He seemed to shimmer in front of my eyes.

"All right," he said. "I've been wanting to do this for a hell of a long time."

A lurid flash of lightning showed me his fist a fraction of a second before it connected. These amateur riders have hands like hams. The lightning seemed to have got inside my skull. I went out.

CHAPTER 7

Benzedrine for Breakfast

I don't suppose that I was unconscious for more than a few minutes. I came to as he was lugging me in through the doorway of a ruined farmhouse. Once inside he dumped me, none too gently, on the earthen floor. I sat up and felt my chin. It hurt.

"I suppose you thought you were being bloody heroic," I said. "They couldn't have followed us in this. I was trying to tell you that when you let fly."

He grinned. He seemed pleased with himself. "I didn't do it because I liked you," he said. "Don't think that."

"Thanks, I didn't imagine you did."

"Stop sparring, you two," her voice cut in. "Roddy, you're far too free with your fists."

"Well, he is too free with his tongue." He grinned again. Undoubtedly he was pleased with himself. I suppose he had reason to be.

Outside the rain came down as if it had been driven from a hose. It was a thick, solid curtain of water. At intervals, like massed gunfire close at hand, the thunder and lightning raged overhead. Like close shelling, too, it was that vicious, personal sort of lightning that made you think it was aimed at yourself. Its flashes showed us clearly our surroundings.

We were in one of those ruined Provençal farmhouses which you find all over that part of the country. There was the remains of a ceiling overhead. Through the gaps in it one could see a roof many of whose tiles were torn and broken. A good deal of the rain was coming down on to us but it was better than being outside.

"How long will this go on?" she asked me.

"It depends," I said. "It might be for hours. You can never tell how long they will last up here."

"What will we do?"

"Stick it out. Try to get some rest." I wasn't feeling particularly well-disposed to either of them just then. I was soaking wet and my jaw hurt. It didn't appear to be broken. That, I suppose, was something. By and large I could have done with being twenty years younger. Taking off my jacket I laid it on the floor beside me. Then I wedged myself into a corner and tried to let my muscles relax. Overhead the storm raged; the lightning stabbed through the empty windows. I did my best to call to mind all the soft luxurious beds I had ever lain on and then to decide which was the best of them. Then I tried to imagine myself on it, sinking into slumber between sheets of the finest linen, with nothing at all to worry about and the world at my command when I awoke. Not a bad dream I thought, in the circumstances, and with the aid of it, after a while, I fell into a sort of uneasy doze. Then, I think, I did go to sleep for a bit.

How long I slept I hadn't the least idea, but when I opened my eyes the storm had gone. Outside the sun was up and blazing. I had an immediate unquiet feeling that I should have stayed awake, that I had delayed our departure beyond the point of safety.

She was sitting opposite to me, her back against the wall, her feet curled under her.

"When did it stop?" I said.

"About an hour ago, I think."

"Why didn't you wake me?"

"I didn't like to. You seemed so whacked."

"Well, thanks. But I don't think we have much time to spare. We must find the car, and we'd better be quick about it." I got to my feet. Every muscle and joint in my body creaked and protested. My wet clothes clung to me. I felt about a hundred. I hated everybody.

Then I saw that young Marston was missing.

The keys of the car were in the pocket of my coat. I reached down and picked it up. The pocket was empty. The keys had gone.

Our eyes met. "It's all right." She answered my unspoken question. "He said he was only going to get some clothes out of the car. He'd leave it for you. He said he'd reach Avignon somehow."

"What then?"

"He's going to Ireland to get the formula back from your wife."

"I hope he finds Mildred in a giving vein," I said grimly.

I went to the doorway and looked out. The countryside was bright and fresh after the storm. The trees of the scrub looked more alive, as if the rain had quenched their thirst, at least for a while. To my left the harsh shapes of the Luberons stood out against the startling blue of the sky.

The farm must once have been a considerable place. It was built of that pink brick common to the country and was bigger than had at first appeared. The house itself was long and low and had numerous out-buildings, now in ruins, built back into the hill behind it. In front of me the terraces of the former vine plantations dropped steeply away before joining the general wilderness.

I did my best to think back over the ground we had

covered last night and the way we had come when we had left the château but, of course, it wasn't much good. Apart from the fact that my recollection was naturally hazy and confused, each of the little valleys in these hills looked just the same as the next one. All I knew for certain was that we were much too close to the château for comfort. I turned back into the room.

"We must find the car," I said. "That's the first essential. And it's time we were off."

She stood up, trying to smooth and pull her soiled and tattered clothes about her. "Roddy left a message for you," she said. "He said if it would do any good he was sorry for knocking you about. And—and, he said I was to tell you to take care of me, that you would do it much better than he could."

I looked at her and something caught me by the throat. Suddenly I didn't hate anyone any more. "I don't know about that," I said. "But I'll try."

As far as I could see there was no one about in the scrub below the terrace, though it was quite impossible to be sure. Behind us we were covered by the house itself and the out-buildings. To our left the ground fell steeply away and I turned to look through the window which commanded this approach. Full in my view about fifty feet below and a hundred yards away was a large clearing. As I stood there I saw the figure of a man come to the edge of the scrub. He paused a moment glancing searchingly to each side and then he crossed the open ground. A sporting rifle was in the crook of his arm; and he was as taut and menacing as a prowling leopard. It was Stuart Jason engaged in his favourite sport—the hunting of man. We hadn't much time, or much distance either, by the look of things.

I turned to her. "Slip down those terraces in front," I said. "When you get to the bottom wait for me. Go as quickly and quietly as you can."

She went over the rough ground like a wraith. When she was safely away I picked up the machine-pistol and followed her.

All I could do was to take a glance at the sun and make a guess at the direction we should take. Then we set out along one of the paths which wound through the scrub. Obviously, with the girl, I could neither make the pace nor take the cuts across country which I had done with Marston the day before. We had, too, to be on the alert for every sound. The sun dried our clothes on us as we went and gradually I began to feel more like a human being. As the minutes passed and no one challenged us I began to hope, too, that we might get away with it. Jason had, after all, been pointing in the opposite direction when I caught that glimpse of him.

Then we had a great stroke of luck. We crossed a ridge and came upon a road. There was only one real road in that locality and that was the one on which we had made our approach yesterday. Ten minutes later we were in sight of the place where I had hidden the car.

There was no other noise save the chirping of the cicadas. Nothing moved in the heat and the stillness. Through the screen of scrub oaks I could just see the top of the car. It looked to be exactly where I had left it. The way to it seemed clear. But I had been at this game before and something told me to go carefully. I made the girl hide in a little hollow beside the path. Then, holding the machine-pistol in front of me, I went on by myself.

Twenty yards from where the car was I slid off the track. Putting my feet down very softly and easing aside the branches and the clinging undergrowth I got myself into a position where I could see the back and both sides of the car. It was as well that I did.

Standing with his back to me was the big brute we had encountered in Arles. He had a whistle in his hand and was in the act of raising it to his lips.

I pushed the machine-pistol forward. The click as it went from safe to fire was quite loud in the stillness.

"Drop that!" I said.

His hand froze six inches from his mouth. His head came round very slowly and I saw his eyes take in the gun. Then his fingers opened and the whistle dropped to the ground.

"Now put your hands up. Right up," I said.

He obeyed slowly.

He was then at my mercy and I was in a quandary. Short of shooting him in the back I didn't see how I was going to render him harmless. I didn't suppose the world would miss him much but just the same I didn't care about the idea. And a shot in that silence would bring the whole pack about my ears. The worst of it was I had a feeling he realized this too. His appearance gave the impression that he was tensed and alert, waiting to take advantage of any mistake I might make, as dangerous as a man in his position can be. What he knew and I knew, though a great many people do not, is that the man behind the gun has his own problems, too.

There was no use wasting time. I had to do something. I went up behind him. As quietly as I could I swung back the gun. I was nothing like quick enough.

He must have been waiting for me. He pivoted like lightning on the balls of his feet, knocked the gun aside as it came down and threw himself on top of me. I hadn't a chance. He was twice my size and four times my weight.

As we fell I kicked out at his crotch. I heard him laugh as he blocked the kick. Then we hit the ground and his weight knocked all my senses awry. His great hands were at my throat and it was as if an iron collar had me from my shoulder to my chin. Someone was turning a screw in it, tightening it. I could feel my eyeballs coming out of my sockets, up and out into a red, roaring mist. The red mist was coagulating and coming down, down, to meet my eyes and scorch them. . . .

Then, suddenly, the great grip relaxed. The huge fingers slackened and slipped off. My eyes cleared for a second and I saw him go suddenly limp and empty. A mute grunt came from his lips, then he fell unconscious beside me.

I couldn't move. I lay there for a full minute taking in great gulps of air and savouring the fact that I was alive. Slowly, my head still whirling, I sat up.

She was standing six feet away, the machine-pistol in her hand. She had belted him on the back of the head with its butt.

"Have I killed him?" She was panting, and looked frightened at what she had done.

I bent over him. There was a long jagged cut on the back of his head from which a thin trickle of blood came. But he was breathing.

"No such luck," I said. "I should think there is nothing but solid bone inside that skull."

There was a wide leather belt round his waist. I ripped this off and secured his arms with it. His bootlaces served to tie up his ankles. Screwing my handkerchief into a ball I rammed it into his mouth. Then I used the free end of the bootlaces to lash his wrists and ankles together. When

Benzedrine for Breakfast

that was done I reckoned I had made as good a parcel of
him as could be managed and I rolled him into the scrub.
He was not going to be particularly comfortable when he
came to, but I didn't see that I should worry on that
account. I turned to her.

"Thanks," I said. "By and large you seem to be taking
care of me at the moment. I shall have to try to repay that
some time."

I leant against the car for a moment or two, then I
opened the driver's door. The key was in the ignition all
right but just now starting the car would wait. There was
something else I wanted very badly.

Reaching in I opened the glove compartment. The
leather case was still where I had put it. Inside were all the
concomitants of twentieth-century living—phenobarbi-
tone, secconal, Gelusil, and the little aluminium box I was
looking for. I shook two of the heart-shaped pills on to my
palm, brought them to my mouth and swallowed them
with a quick shake of my head. An hour to work and six
hours working, was what they said. With me it was usually
shorter and longer. That should see me through all right.

For some reason I had not wanted her to see me taking
them. When I turned to look for her she was standing
with her back to me. Her eyes were on the place where I
had rolled the big thug.

"Come on," I said. "Time to go."

"Can we leave him there like that?"

"Yes. Someone will find him. The bad die hard. We can
send Jason a postcard from Nice."

She got in beside me. I started the engine, and drove
out on to the road. Then I pointed the car back the way we
had come.

"Where are we going?" she asked.

"Nice. To put you on to an aeroplane for home."

We were over the crest with our speed mounting. At that time in the morning and in those lonely places there was likely to be little traffic. I was chancing the corners and letting her go.

And round the second of two fast curves three men were pushing a farm cart across the road.

I couldn't have stopped even if I had wanted to. As it happened I did not, for I had seen the fourth man standing on a rock directing operations. He had a sawn-off shotgun in his hand.

I put my near-side wheels on the grass verge, prayed it would hold and pushed down my foot. There was a medley of shouts and I saw the men laying their shoulders savagely to the cart. I thought I heard the boom of a shotgun and something spattered against the steel roof.

The right front wing hit the projecting back of the cart. The whole cart exploded in front of my eyes. Pieces of wood and earth and old iron flew about in front of the bonnet and something went scraping and smashing down the side of the car. Then we were through. I heard the shotgun give another futile boom as we left them and went into the next curve.

We were going much too fast. I had had to cram on speed to get by the cart and now I couldn't lose it in time. Everything was wrong—speed, line, positioning. I slammed on the brakes and swung the wheel hard over. It was all I could do.

The brakes bit and held; the big saloon swayed and wallowed. The tyres scrabbled on the rough road and voiced their protest as she slid. I kicked on the throttle as the back came round. She heeled again like a ship in the seaway; then she straightened and the corner was behind us.

"Four wheel drift," I said. "Very badly executed. That, I fear, has torn it."

"Why?"

I cursed myself for not holding my tongue. She had been through enough as it was without frightening her again. But in my mind had been the image of the red Ferrari. They would be told our way by the men with the cart and it should not take them long to get after me. There was no escape in these mountains, nowhere we could turn off and hope to lose them. We must only take the road ahead and make the most of it while we could. Once more my foot went down.

But before Lourmarin a bright red dot leapt like an angry bee into my driving mirror. It grew bigger at a fantastic speed. Once again I wondered who was driving it.

There was no chance of out-distancing them. We simply had not got the speed to do it. Even with cars which were evenly matched I doubted if I could hold the artist who drove the other car. I didn't much like admitting this to myself but it was true. That being so we should have to try something else.

" 'Whatever happens we have got the maxim gun which they have not'," I said with a cheerfulness I was far from feeling. "Give it to me, will you?"

She picked the machine-pistol from the floor between us and laid it across my knees. Leaning across I wound the window beside her down to its fullest extent. All the time I kept one eye firmly fixed on the driving mirror. The image of the Ferrari was getting bigger and bigger. I had a plan of sorts and part of it was to delay them as long as possible. This meant doing all I could with the car and keeping the gun steady on my knees and ready to my hand at the same time. It wasn't easy driving.

"Get down on the floor underneath the dash," I said to her. "And stay there."

I guessed that Jason was in the Ferrari. He would want to make this catch himself. I also guessed, from what I had seen and heard of him, that Jason's mind was back at Balaclava. His method of attack would be the charge, lances down, pennons flying. Jason, I reckoned, had plenty of dash and very little brains. He would want to show off before the girl, too. That was a certainty. Let me just read his character right, and I thought I had a chance of beating him. It would be pure pleasure to do so. Once more I took the gun off safe.

They came with a rush when they did come, shouldering me over to the side of the road. I trod on the brakes and came up all standing. The Ferrari overshot me by a fraction which gave me about two seconds. They were enough. I slid across the seat and pushed the machine-pistol through the window.

The near-side door of the Ferrari flew open and Jason leaped into the road. In his hand was a World War I Webley ·45, the sort of weapon he would carry. He was all dash and drama. "Out into the road, you two," he barked as soon as his feet hit the surface, "and be quick about it!"

"Not so fast, Jason," I said. "Drop that gun or I'll cut you in two." I would have, too, that was the hell of it. The horrible craving to hear death chattering out in front of me had gripped me again.

I think he knew what he was up against, I think he heard it in my voice.

He had a chance, but it was a very small one, of getting his antiquated weapon to bear before my slugs struck him. Our eyes met across the six feet of road between us. The sights of the machine-pistol were on his chest, and he had to make a decision and make it fast. Faster perhaps than he thought because the lust to kill was welling so hard and strong inside me I could scarcely control it. I could feel my lips gaping back into a grin. My finger took up the first soft pressure. There was now only a hair's-breadth between him and eternity.

Then he dropped the gun.

I heard my breath go out in a long, high sigh as if it had been another man's. For a second or two I said nothing as I fought for and regained control over myself.

"Kick the gun over to the side of the road," I told him, "and put up your hands." I raised my voice. "Come out from behind the wheel," I called to the other occupant of the car. "And don't come carrying anything."

"It's all right, Simon," said a voice I recognized from over the years. "I am in the driving department, not the fighting one." A man came smiling round the front of the car with his hands held away from his body.

I nearly dropped the machine-pistol. All at once I was back in the thirties, a hero-worshipping boy, drinking *campari* at Monza with a slim little Italian who had just been given a place in the Alfa team.

"Toni!" I exclaimed. "Toni Velletti! I knew there was an artist driving that car. It's no disgrace to be taken by you. What is she like to drive?"

"She is a sweet job—one of the three litres. There is a Bugatti Royale up at the house, Simon, you ought to see it."

"You wretched, gutless wop!" Jason's clipped, arrogant voice cut in. "God, the trash I have to serve me. . . ."

"The negroes commence at Calais, don't they, Colonel?" I said. "You have strange ideas of inspiring loyalty." I turned to Veletti. "I'll have to stop you coming after me, Toni," I said. "Pull the valves out of the tyres, will you?"

Veletti gave me a strange smile. "A wretched gutless wop could scarcely do other than assist the man with the gun, Simon," he said.

It only took him a few minutes. "Don't get between me and Jason," I told him as he came towards me with them. When I had them I let out the clutch and pushed home the gear lever. I didn't take my eyes off Jason. He was as dangerous as a cornered wild animal. Come to think of it that is just about what he was. Then I trod on the throttle and we shot off down the road.

I turned to the left in Cadenet. I knew we could make time over the gently rolling slopes through the cornfields on the north bank of the river. So we came to the Pont de Mirabeau. Beyond it, where the road runs along the edge of the cliff, I stopped the car.

The storm had put the Durance in spate and the waters were swirling past thirty feet below in a muddy, tawny flood. Taking the machine-pistol by the butt I threw it into space. It hit the water with a little splash and disappeared.

I walked slowly back to the car. I felt empty, drained, like a man who has been through a catharsis. I knew what it was—I had been purged of the lust to kill. I wasn't a bit proud of the way I had felt and I was glad to be rid of the tommy-gun.

When I reached the car I found her huddled into a corner of the seat. She had not spoken since we had left Jason and Veletti and, taken up with other thoughts, I had scarcely noticed her silence. Her eyes were huge in her face; her skin was paper thin, and white with strain and fatigue. Her teeth were clamped over her lower lip. She looked at me as one looks at a complete stranger—a stranger one neither likes nor trusts. Then she turned her glance away, quickly.

I got into the car and took the road for Rians. It is much straighter than it looks on the map and I knew I could cover it pretty fast. It would take me on to N.7 which was where I wanted to get and where I could really make time.

"You would have killed him" she said, almost in a whisper. "You wanted to. I heard it in your voice."

"It was a bluff. It was him or us. It worked, didn't it?"

"You didn't know it was going to work. You might have had to shoot."

"Jason is the sort of soldier you point in the right direction and hope for the best. When you come up against him you give him a push and point him in another way. That is why he never made more than a half-colonel of cavalry. It had to work."

"You hate him don't you?"

"I hate what he stands for. I hate arrogance and ruthlessness. I've seen too much of them."

"You can be pretty ruthless yourself."

"I haven't the fascist assumption that because I commanded a crack cavalry regiment and got two D.S.O.'s in the Desert there is one set of rules for me and another for everyone else."

"Does he think that? Perhaps his manner is only a front. People aren't all what they have in the shop window, are they? And he did have a series of bad breaks."

"So have a lot of other people. You seem to have changed your mind about him."

"Well, I have, a bit. He was really, oh, I don't know, charming is not the word—gallant I suppose it is, when

I was at the château. He was in charge there. He could have done well, anything. Yet whenever I saw him he was kind. I was terrified all the time I was there except when he came. Kindness when you are frightened is quite something after all."

I felt a familiar knot forming inside my stomach. I recognized it and cursed it and myself and the situation I was in. It was the same hard knot that had formed inside me when I found that Mildred was sleeping around with the racing boys.

We threaded through the streets of St. Maximim and out on to the great main highway to the Coast. I pushed the speed into the nineties and held it there. We drove on in silence. I had a lot—too much—to think about. She sat beside me staring out through the windscreen. She had pulled her borrowed shirt—it was mine, I remembered—about her and was trying to do something with her hair. I was all too conscious of her presence. I wanted to get to Nice, to get her to safety and to get out of the tangle I had got myself into.

As we ran through Brignoles she said, "Couldn't we stop for breakfast or coffee or something? I'm famished. Isn't there a good hotel somewhere here?"

"It's off the road." I looked at my watch. "No, I'm sorry, we'll be put to the pin of our collar to make it as it is."

"Very well then. We're practically airborne now, any way. It shouldn't take much longer, I suppose."

"I'd stop if I could," I said. "But we just can't spare the time. It is all right where we are now but from Fréjus to Nice can be a nightmare even at this hour. You never know how much time you'll lose. That's why I'm cramming on. Can you stick it?"

"I'll manage."

I looked at her. Tiredness and exhaustion were written all over her. "You poor kid," I said. "You've been getting it hard." I rummaged in the glove compartment and found the little box. "Here," I said. "Take one of those. It'll keep you going."

"What are they?"

"Pep pills. Advisable in an emergency, but not as a diet."

"I suppose this ranks as an emergency. I won't wake up in Buenos Aires, will I?"

"Not unless you want to."

She didn't make any bones about it. It was one of the things I liked about her. At the château I had wrongly accused her of being missish. There was nothing remotely missish in her. She took one of the pills and swallowed it. "Benzedrine for breakfast," she said. "My word, I am living it up."

"It isn't benzedrine, but it will keep you going until I put you on to the aircraft."

"What are you going to do then?"

"I'm going to a tiny place in the hills behind Cannes where I have what Mildred calls a villa but I call a cottage. It's a relic of my bachelor days. There is a married couple nearby who will look after me; I have a bag full of books in the back of the car. I am going to sleep and eat and drink wine and lie in the sun, and, sometime, think out what I'm going to do with the rest of my life."

"Then Roddy and I won't see you again?"

"Not unless we run across one another in London."

"Will they do anything to us?"

"Who? Mantovelli and Co.?"

"Yes."

"I can't say. I don't know enough about what is in that envelope or how valuable it is to them." And then some devil made me add: "But if they do I have no doubt that Colonel Jason will be most gallant."

For once we had a clear run across the Esterels. Only one *camion* held me up and that just for a minute or two. So we came into Cannes with quite a bit in hand. The traffic, too, between Cannes and Antibes, seemed lighter than usual. I made up time hand over fist, and at this rate reckoned to have something to spare in Nice. We should need it, too. Obviously she would have to get fresh clothes before she flew to London.

"How long more?" she said.

I watched a grand sport Salmson fill my driving mirror, essay to pass and then fall away as I fed more throttle.

"Fifteen minutes at this rate."

"This is good-bye, then."

"Yes."

"Then it doesn't matter, but I just want to know. Why did you stop driving?"

"There are too many reasons to tell you that in fifteen minutes."

"Your right shoe is built up. Has that anything to do with it?"

"You are very observant. It is only five-eighths of an inch."

"I saw it while you were asleep at the farmhouse."

"What do you know about my driving? It all happened when you were in the nursery."

"What Mantovelli told me. He knows everything about you. That is how they got on to your aunt at Aix. He is interested in you. He has your press-cuttings."

"What!"

"He showed them to me at the château. You had a crash at Le Mans in 1949, and broke your thigh."

A millionaire, I reflected, would have no difficulty in getting press-cuttings about anyone he wanted and getting them quickly. It was all in character. Mantovelli would want to learn what he could about a possible adversary. He had a reputation for thoroughness; this bore it out.

"It was at the Esses," I said. "I came in too fast and on the wrong line."

We let the rest of it hang there—the lop-sided feeling I had had when I came out of hospital, the attempts I had made to drive again, the way I had been out of tune with my car at speed, the hopeless hash I had made of my corners and finally the sick realization that my touch and my nerve had gone. For once I had been good. I could say that without conceit because I knew it and anyway it was written in the results. Some people can get into a car and by merely driving it can make it go quicker than the rest. There is no explanation of this just as there is no explanation of any other God-sent gift. It's a combination, I suppose, of judgment, timing and reflex action, and you either have it or you have not. It's as simple as that. For a little while I had been amongst the few. The sweet smell of success had been in my nostrils though it did not stay there very long. An invitation to drive in a works team was on its way when I had piled my Aston up. After that —*finis* and the realization that I had to live with myself for the rest of my life.

It was she who broke the silence. "I wonder", she said, "if you are going to get away from us so easily."

"What do you mean?"

"I think you are in this with us now and you can't run away. Mantovelli will send Jason after Roddy and they

will keep after him until they get what they want. Mantovelli has got what he wants all his life and he doesn't care
how he gets it. And you have interfered with his plans.
You know too much. You'll be on their list, too. Roddy
doesn't even begin to know how to fight them. Please
help us. You might as well."

"You don't want help from an old dead-beat like me."

"You're not a dead-beat. You proved it back there."

"Your brother hates the sight of me."

"Only because you won't let him like you. Why won't
you let people like you, Simon?" She laid her hand on my
arm. "Look, back there in the woods you said you owed
me something. Now I'm asking for payment."

I tightened my lips. Come what may I was not going to
get drawn any further into this. "No," I said. "From here
on you are on your own."

"I see. Then I do despise you. You are running away.
And all the time you will be waiting for Jason to come
after you. Because that is what he'll do. You've humiliated
him and he is not going to forget it. Sooner or later he'll
catch up with you."

"Jason is getting older every year like the rest of us.
He'll get gout or thrombosis or cirrhosis of the liver.
Give him time and he'll forget. Besides, Mantovelli keeps
him too busy. He won't have time to bother about me."

"He won't forget and you know it. Next time he'll
prove to himself that he is better than you. He's got to.
That is how he's made. He must be the best there is. Look,
Simon, he was kind to me in the château and I'm grateful
to him for that, but don't think that has blinded me to
what he is. I don't think he is rotten right through as you
do, but I know he is cruel and vengeful and no one must
be allowed to hurt him without suffering for it."

Benzedrine for Breakfast

We came in along the Promenade des Anglais. I turned to the left by the Hotel Ruhl and then pulled up outside one of those smart women's shops in the Avenue de Verdun. I switched off the engine. The heat came up to meet us and the bustle and roar of the traffic rose and eddied about us. I didn't look at her.

"Don't you see, Simon," I heard her saying. "You can't go on running away. You hate yourself, don't you, for something that happened when you were driving? You'll hate yourself worse if you stay out of this."

"You'll want some clothes for the aircraft," I said. "Go in there and get them. There is money in the glove box in front of you. Take what you think you'll need."

"And what am I going to say to them, I'd like to know," she said crossly. "I look like a character out of the Rape of the Sabine women."

Then I did look at her. Colour had come back to her cheeks and in fact she looked remarkably well—as well, that is to say, as a woman can who has slept and fought and travelled in a man's shirt and trousers and nothing else. "From what I can see," I said, "and from where I sit I can see pretty well, I wouldn't put you down as that type."

"Well!"

"Tell them", I said, "that you have been out with an Englishman who has been trying to acquire the Gallic touch. They'll understand."

There was colour in her cheeks all right, now, and in her eyes too. She slammed the door of the Bentley in a way that made even that big car shake, and stalked across the pavement into the shop. An elderly American in a Palm Beach suit who had been standing by the car took off his hat and grinned sympathetically at me.

I was smiling as I drove around to the air station. As

I walked up to the counter I felt lighter-hearted than I had done for months. I suppose I was grinning like a fool for the clerk smiled gaily back at me. Yes, M'sieu, he said, he had a cancellation. But as a matter of fact, the aircraft was not full, there were a few seats available.

"Two will do," I said and paid for them.

I had made even better time than I thought so I took a suitcase from the back of the car and went round to a barber whom I knew. He shaved me and tidied me up and I borrowed a room and a shower from him. By the time I had stood under the shower for a bit with the cold tap on full blast, and towelled myself dry and put on fresh clothes I was a different man.

When I got back she was sitting on a chair to the right of the door looking at *Paris Match*. For a second I quite failed to recognize her. Then she stood up beside me with a rustle.

They had fitted her out with a flared green skirt belted wide at the waist, and plain white blouse. Someone had done something with her hair and her face had been touched with what make-up it needed. That was all, but it was enough. I caught my breath.

"It's generally considered rude to stare," she said demurely.

I didn't say anything. I took her by the arm and led her to a café a few doors up. We sat inside at the bar, away from the blinding heat. I ordered brandy in large glasses and half a bottle of champagne. When they came I made the cocktails myself. Lifting my glass I touched it to the rim of hers.

"Here's to us," I said.

She gave a little sigh. "Yes," she said. "But why?"

I felt in my pocket and took out the two tickets. I laid

them on the counter between us. "I'm coming with you," I said.

"Oh, Simon!!" It was payment indeed to see her face light up.

"And, just for the record," I said, "I made up my mind in the aircraft station—before I saw you looking like something out of the Rue de la Paix. For the record again, now that I have, there are no regrets at all."

An hour later we were in the aircraft climbing towards the Alps.

CHAPTER 7

Poste Restante

At London Airport I put her into a taxi, gave the driver the address in Brompton Square and told her to stay there until she heard from me. I hoped the hunt had switched to her brother but I wasn't taking any chances. For all I knew any of those innocuous-looking returning holiday-makers who had filled our plane might be members of Mantovelli's establishment detailed to watch us. His organization was efficient and his net was wide. It had come as a surprise to say the least of it to find Veletti amongst his men.

Toni Veletti had been one of the star drivers in the Alfa team in the thirties, a likeable and unassuming little Italian with magic in his hands. He would be too old now to drive in the *Grandes Épreuves*, of course, and racing drivers, like professional boxers and steeplechase riders, the practitioners of those sports which take men apart, have not much left to them once their youth has gone, if they survive it. Thinking of Veletti and myself and of young Marston on the threshold of it all I got on to an escalator and went to look for a plane to Dublin.

I got a seat without much difficulty and, once we were airborne, I shut my eyes and began to try to think things out.

I was now committed, there was no going back. Once I had accepted that fact it remained to decide what I was going to do and how I was going to do it. Obviously the first thing was to find Mildred and to get the envelope from her or to help young Marston to get it. This might not be all that easy for if Mildred was in one of her moods she was unlikely to be helpful to me or to anyone she thought came from me. Still, there were one or two persuaders I could use if it came to a pinch. I rather thought I could manage Mildred—if I could find her. She might be almost anywhere in Ireland racketing around the race meetings with the Dunmanway set.

I asked the hostess for an Irish newspaper and, when she brought it, turned to the racing page. There had been a meeting at the Curragh this afternoon. That meant that the Dunmanways and their hangers-on were probably within a reasonable radius of Dublin, so I should not have very much difficulty in locating Mildred.

I began to wonder, then, where young Marston had got to or if he had got away at all. If they had caught up with him the envelope would be a useful card in my hands to guarantee his safety.

There did not seem to be much use in planning further ahead. For once I had the envelope in my possession I was determined to find out what was in it. That, at least, would be the price of my participation. It contained a formula of some sort; that much they had let slip. But what that formula was, what it affected and why it meant so much to Mantovelli were things I had made up my mind I was going to be told. I had several guesses running around in my head, but they were guesses and no more. Basically I knew as little as when I had held the envelope in my hands that night at Arles.

There was a bit of a hold-up over Collinstown. The weather was closing in and we were delayed. By the time we were down and through the Customs it was late enough. There seemed to be no point in starting off enquiries then, I was tired and hungry and I went straight to the club.

The first person I saw when I entered the bar was Maurice Kenway. He was sitting on one of the cushioned benches under the Spy cartoon. There was a gin and tonic in front of him and in his hands was one of those Dublin evening newspapers which never seem to contain much except the racing results and what the solicitor said to the District Justice. He was quite alone and looked extremely bored. I was glad enough to see him. He would know Mildred's whereabouts if anyone did.

"I thought you were in the south of France, Simon," he said as I approached.

"I was. I was looking for you as a matter of fact. They told me you had left."

"I had a runner in the Gallinules so I came back to see him. I'm only here for a day or two."

"How is the villa going?"

"Not too bad. It's costing rather more than I thought."

"It always does."

"I wonder if I should have gone to Jamaica."

"Why not. You could have bought a Chevrolet Bel Air like Noel Coward."

"What on earth is that?"

"It's a sort of motor-car, Maurice. Have you seen anything of Mildred? Was she at the Curragh?"

Maurice coughed tactfully and looked at his drink. "Someone said she was but I didn't see her," he said. "Look, Simon, I don't know whether you are going to like this, but Mildred, I'm told, has been going yackety yack-yack about you to some purpose since you went away. She is supposed to be on her way to London to get a divorce."

"Well, it's nice to know what is going on. When is she off?"

"I can't say. She may be there by now for all I know."

"Where is she living nowadays?"

"I haven't heard. I'm only just back myself."

"Well, you seem to have done very well in the time. She won't be at home at Newlands anyway. It's shut up."

I kept quiet for a bit then for I wanted to think things out. Although it seemed as if a hundred years had passed it was in fact only about thirty-six hours since Aunt Dorothy had posted the letter. If it had arrived at all it was in all probability still lying at Newlands or in the local post-office. If so I could collect it from either of these places without interference from Mildred. On the other hand she might have left a forwarding address. In London, I remembered, she usually stayed with a friend of her youth, a flash woman columnist on one of the sultrier daily papers who had a flat in Eaton Place. If the letter had been forwarded I supposed I should have to follow her to London and get it from her there.

"Shall we dine here?" Maurice's voice broke into my thoughts. "It's rather too late to go out. We can have a bottle of the Nuits St. George. It's very good."

Later, when our food and wine were before us, he said to me, "There is an extraordinary story going around about the young Marstons. You remember him—that young chap I pointed out to you at Mantovelli's party?"

I nodded. I wondered what was coming.

"It seems Marston was to meet Legarde, the American owner, you know the chap I'm sure, he won the Two

Thousand Guineas and the Prix de l'Arc de Triomphe last year."

"I don't," I said, "but go on."

"It was some business deal and they were to put it through in Cannes. What business deal Roddy Marston could have had on which would interest Legarde I can't think but that is by the way. Marston never turned up. Legarde phoned his hotel about fifty times, called up everyone he could think of, even rang the old General in Brompton Square. But the boy had disappeared. The only thing Legarde got out of the General was that Sue, his sister, was with him. She has gone, too."

"Who told you all this?"

"That horse-coping R.A.F. chap. Can't remember his name. He goes around everywhere—I'm sure you have met him."

"I don't think so, but it doesn't matter. Go on, Maurice."

"He was having a drink with some people I knew at the Curragh. He was full of it. It seems he is rather a chum of Legarde's. Apparently Legarde had been on the phone to him about it. Said he was properly steamed up. Of course there may be nothing in it. But it's strange because it's true, apparently, that no one has seen them."

"You are not quite right there, Maurice," I said. "I have for one. So has Stuart Jason."

"What!"

I dug out a piece of Stilton and spread it. Rightly or wrongly I had made up my mind to take Maurice into my confidence. He had been a good friend to me in Hannah's and pretty well the only friend I had during my time in Ireland among the horses. He was a bit of an old gossip, but then so are most of us at heart. He liked to do himself well, too well, those who laughed at him maintained, but

then again, so would most of us if we could afford it, and
Maurice's American grandmother had seen to it that he
could. He was steady in a crisis as I knew for I had been
in more than one with him. It looked now, too, as if I
should need his help, for I wanted to go down to Kildare
quickly tomorrow and possibly over to England immediately afterwards. Also, heaven alone knew what
story Jason might seek to put about concerning the
Marstons, concerning especially Sue, to use as a weapon
to attain his ends. It was as well that someone besides myself should know the truth.

"Hang on to your hat, Maurice," I said to him. "It's
quite a story."

And there and then, over our port, I told it to him. I
also told him what I proposed to do.

"I see," he said when I had finished. "And, tomorrow,
I take it you'll want transport?"

"That's it, Maurice."

"Well, you can count on me."

"Thanks, I thought I could."

Maurice had a Mark VIII Jaguar with automatic transmission. In this, next morning, we drove down to Kildare.
The automatic transmission suited Maurice as it does a
lot of those flying fellows who don't care about cars you
have to drive. All he had to do was to turn the wheel or
press the pedal at appropriate or inappropriate moments.
It left him plenty of time to gossip about his friends. It
also drove him much better than he would have driven
himself but it wasn't much fun for me. I have a feeling that
he knew this for there was the slightest of sly grins on his
face most of the way down. As we ambled along the Naas
road at eighty he asked me if I would care to drive.

"No thanks," I said. "I suppose you have a cocktail bar and a washing machine in the back?"

"No, dear boy, only a telly," he said with a chuckle.

He loaned her to me to go over to Newlands. I was to return for lunch and we were to fly to London that afternoon.

I let myself in with my key. The house had the vaguely damp and musty air all unoccupied houses have. There was a pile of letters on the table in the hall; none of them was of any interest whatsoever. I fired the whole lot into a plate bucket which we used as a waste-paper basket. Then I went upstairs.

In my dressing-room I unlocked one of the twin top drawers of my chest of drawers and pulled it open. What I was looking for was there all right, wrapped in oiled silk, at the back of the drawer underneath a pile of handkerchiefs. I took off the wrapping and looked at the workmanlike revolver in my hand. It was a Smith and Wesson ·38 Military and Police model. An American colonel had got it for me during the war. Like lots of others I had been looking for a Lüger. The colonel, who had been doing some sort of liaison job with us at the time, was a crack shot and a pistol expert and I had told him that I wanted a Lüger. "I don't wonder you fellows want to throw away the things you are issued with," he had said in tones of the utmost contempt. "But say, listen, don't go getting a Lüger either. It's the most over-rated, talked-up weapon in existence. It's badly balanced, prone to jam and darn difficult to shoot straight. What sells it is its looks, and glamour ain't no good in a gun. I'll get you a weapon you'll have a chance of hitting something with."

He had been as good as his word and now I held it in my hand. He had taught me a little about using it, too.

"It's a close-combat weapon," he had said. "But so they all are when the chips are down. Anyone who tries to hit home with a revolver at a greater range than the width of a room wants his head examined. Unless of course he is an expert—like me. And it took me twenty years to learn the way to do it."

There was a box of ammunition, too. I opened it, emptied a pile of the cartridges into a handkerchief and tied the four corners together. Then I took a raincoat from my wardrobe and put the cartridges into one pocket and the revolver into another. They would have made unwieldy bulges in the pockets of my suit and I had no wish to be caught by the customs carrying lethal weapons.

I threw the coat over the back of the chair. Moved by an impulse I went into the big, airy bedroom we had shared, on and off, through seven stormy years of marriage. Immediately I noticed something.

Mildred had been back. Beside her bed before, there had been the books she liked to read when she did read. The Fox-Hunting Man, I remembered, Ernest Thompson Seton from her childhood, Somerville and Ross and some others. They were gone. I opened her wardrobe. It was empty. On her dressing-table had been a photograph which she particularly prized. It had been taken when she won a lady's race somewhere in England beating one of those pot-hunting women pro's by a neck. It, too, was gone. The emptiness of the room spelled finality. Not that I had ever expected—or wanted—anything else. But there is always some sadness in an ending.

Then I remembered that all the letters in the hall had been for me. Mildred had taken her own mail if there had been any. So if the envelope had arrived from Aunt Dorothy she had got it. On the other hand it might just possibly be still in the post office, for Mrs. Rogers, the post-mistress, had a way of her own with letters. Knowing we were away she might well have stopped delivery without waiting for instructions.

There was an extension telephone beside the bed. I picked it up intending to ask Mrs. Rogers if she had any post for us. The line was dead. I remembered then that the bill would have come in in my absence and it was probable that I had been cut off, or, again, Mrs. Rogers might have done it herself. I ran downstairs and out to the car.

The local post office is a tiny little shop in the main street of the village of Courtnagay. It is chiefly given over to selling groceries, sweets, newspapers and pretty well everything under the sun. Indeed the only thing which tells you that it is in fact a post office is a green tin sign fixed to its wall bearing in yellow letters the Irish words *Oifig An Phoist*.

Mrs. Rogers was delighted to see me. She is a stout motherly female who is a very good friend and a very bad enemy as those who have fought with her in the matter of trunk calls have found out to their cost. If she doesn't like you there is wont to be an unavoidable delay of considerable length in getting a call and when it does come it is subject to frequent interruptions often from Mrs. Rogers herself. However, I was one of the fortunate ones and she was prepared to turn a blind eye to all and every form of rule and regulation of the post office service for those whom she liked. It was said that she had been known to steam open other people's letters if one of her favourites wanted to know what was inside, but the truth of this I never heard tested.

"Glory be to God, Mr. Herald," she greeted me. "I thought you'd left us for good. Sure that's why I started to keep the letters for ye and cut off the telephone. There's no sense in him paying them bills for half the countryside and the men on the farm for to be using it on ye, I says. An' ye just missed herself. She was in this morning. That is if ye wanted to see her." Mrs. Rogers sniffed. Mildred was not one of her favourites.

"Was she, Mrs. Rogers, and did she get any post, I wonder?"

"She did an' all. And in a raw red tearin' hurry she was too, for she was catching the plane for London, so she said." Mrs. Rogers sniffed again.

"And her post, Mrs. Rogers?" I asked.

"Ah sure it was nothing. Only a big old envelope with a lot of them furrin' stamps on it. Will ye take yours, sir?"

"Yes, thanks, Mrs. Rogers, I might as well." I took the letters which she handed me and stuffed them into my pocket. So Mildred had got the envelope. I said good-bye to the post-mistress and went out to the car.

Maurice was in his study mixing Guinness and champagne.

"Mildred has the letter. She left for London this morning," I said to him.

"I see. Have some of this. It'll do you good. I suppose you want to get after her."

"Yes."

"All right. We'll have lunch immediately. I told them you might be in a hurry."

An hour later we landed at Dublin Airport. Maurice took his brief case and his slide rule and all the other appurtenances of modern private flying into the control tower to get the weather and his final clearances.

I sat on in the Apache for a bit and then, reflecting that if the weather was good I should be bored and if it was

Poste Restante

bad I should be terrified, I decided to buy myself something to read on the trip. As I strolled across the apron I saw a Viscount coming in to land and in the main hall the loud-speakers were announcing the arrival of a flight from Paris.

I bought *The Times* and a copy of the *Autocar* and was glancing along the rows of paper-backs when I heard the Paris passengers coming through. Idly I looked up to watch them. There were the usual assortment of American tourists, business men, some returning holiday-makers and an obvious honeymoon couple. Then, suddenly, I opened *The Times* and buried my face in it.

There had been no mistaking that tall, commanding, arrogant figure. Stuart Jason was striding across the hall. The hunt was up again and close on my heels.

CHAPTER 8

The Lady is a Tramp

I moved down one side of the bookstall where I could watch him with little likelihood of being detected. He went into one of the telephone booths. After a few minutes he came out again and stood for a moment frowning, apparently undecided what to do. Then he beckoned imperiously to a uniformed attendant. As the man approached he took what appeared to be an aircraft ticket out of his pocket and showed it to him. The attendant looked at it, said something and pointed. Jason crossed the hall with long strides and went upstairs.

I put *The Times* under my arm and went out to the aircraft. There I waited in a fever of impatience for Maurice to join me. At last he came walking across the concrete. He opened the door and climbed in.

"Jason's here," I said.

"Is he?" He was busy securing the door. "They don't waste much time, do they? Did you find out what he was up to?"

"He was on the blower. Then he went upstairs. They must have picked me up. It would have been easy enough. They have probably been to Mrs. Rogers by now and found out that Mildred has left for London. I must say that the more I see of these people the more I'm impressed with their efficiency."

"There isn't a London service for a couple of hours or so. And he has got to get on to it."

"That is probably what he is at right now. We've a bit of a start. Fly downhill all the way, will you?"

"I'll try. Depends on the weather how we go." He pressed a switch and called the tower for his runway and his taxi clearance. Then he moved his hand on the throttles; the twin engines gripped her and we started out to our take-off position.

For a private aircraft the Apache is, I suppose, fairly sizeable, but she seemed like a fly on that vast runway. When we got out Maurice ran his engines up and tested his magnetos. Then he called the tower again.

"Clear to take off!" came crackling through the loud-speakers in the cabin.

We moved into position and pointed down the great concrete path. Then we were hurtling along it, the tail came up and the twin engines lifted her. Maurice reported that we were airborne, and it seemed only a matter of seconds before we were over Bray Head and pointing south-east.

The weather was good. There was blazing sunshine and the ceiling was somewhere in pale blue hazy infinity. We climbed to nine thousand feet and stayed there.

I settled back in my seat, listened to the chatter of the airline operators in the loudspeakers, and waited for the Welsh mountains to come up. "Tell me about Stuart Jason," I said.

"He is everything they say he is—he's a bully and a sadist. But he is full of guts. The hotter it is the better he likes it. He's dangerous. Don't underestimate him. He has charm, too, when he wants to use it."

"He's a fool."

"Perhaps, but he has a certain animal cunning. And he has Mantovelli's brains behind him now. It is the old man who is pulling the strings and Jason is jumping to them. Don't forget that."

"Someone once told me that Mantovelli has a medieval mind. Jason's been fortunate. He's found the right master."

"Luneberg Heath came too soon for him. Killing is his business. He wants another war."

"Maybe he has got one."

We left the Welsh mountains and I opened the *Autocar*. Le Mans was next week and all the usual *marques* had teams entered. I read the pre-race news and then, because it all brought certain hopes and fears much too vividly back to me, I closed the magazine and began to look about me.

The trouble about travelling in light aircraft is that you can see straight ahead into the weather. This doubtful pleasure is denied you on commercial airliners and an excellent thing too. All the warning you have of bad weather in an airliner is a brief broadcast telling you to fasten your seat belt and then your whisky and soda jumps into your lap, the whole outfit drops about sixty feet and you are into it. In a light aircraft you can see the front building up before you for miles. That was what was happening now.

A mass of thick cloud, black as the inside of a coal bucket, stretched slap across the horizon. Its base, as far as I could make out, was right on the ground so there was no possibility of going underneath it. Above it, angry looking lumps of cloud of a slightly lighter colour were building up into fantastic shapes of mountain peaks and valleys. Nearer us was a thin, transparent curtain of rain. Very soon we began to get this on the windscreen and Maurice set the wipers going.

"What do you propose to do about all that," I said.

"About what?"

The Lady is a Tramp

"About that bloody awful-looking collection of destruction and the wrath of God immediately ahead."

"Oh, that. Go through it, of course. It's not very deep."

"Thank you very much," I said. "I think I shall go to sleep."

"I thought you were a barbiturate addict and couldn't sleep."

"That is one of Mildred's stories. Don't believe it or any others of them for that matter."

"There is a paper bag beside you in the pocket."

"I won't need it," I said with dignity. "I'm just pure honest-to-God terrified. Why don't you carry a steward and a bottle of brandy?"

Maurice laughed. "Fasten your seat belt," he said. "Here we go."

I shut my eyes. My seat fell out from under me and left me sitting on air. Then it came back again and hit me a crack on the bottom which sent me flying to the roof. For the next ten minutes we performed every conceivable evolution except turning over and flying on our back. I am not at all certain that we did not do that as well for I only opened my eyes once throughout. When I did so it was to see Maurice, looking a bit grim, both hands on the wheel, his eyes firmly fixed on his blind-flying instruments. It seemed to be taking him all his time to fly the thing. I shut my eyes once more and tried to imagine myself safely in a fast car somewhere in France.

Then at last we were out into comparatively clear air. Maurice looked at his map and his watch and called up London Airport to tell them he was crossing the boundary.

"You all right?" he asked as he put the handpiece down. "It was a little bumpy."

The Lady is a Tramp

"Was it?" I said. "I didn't notice. I was fast asleep."

"You sleep very restlessly. I'm sorry for your girl friends."

I let that one go. "And you", I said, "do this sort of thing for pleasure?"

"What of it? Some people drive fast cars for pleasure. Bloody lunatics, I call them. No road accidents in the sky."

"No, and no brakes either. Christ, there is another of them coming up."

This time I shut my eyes and kept them shut. Although the turbulence lasted longer it was nothing like so intense. I suppose I did catnap for a bit. Some time later a fair amount of concentrated chatter in the loudspeakers, apparently directed at us, made me sit up and look about me.

We were in the middle of a dense cloud which was swirling past the windows in grey, wispy eddies. The aircraft was banked over, Maurice was frowning at his instruments and someone was nattering something in the speakers about a rate one turn.

"What the hell is going on now?" I enquired. "In fog on the road we always put on our lights and slow down. I must say——"

"Simon, I like you a lot," Maurice said tersely. "And we'll have a splendid giggle about this over dinner later on. But right now I'm being talked down into Croydon, so pack it up for the present, will you?"

A moment later we were under the cloud base and over the acceleration strips. Then Maurice dropped her on the grass as lightly as thistledown, the brakes caught and held her and we were down.

"Very nice, too," I said.

Maurice looked at his watch as we taxied over to the

airport buildings. "A bit late, I'm afraid," he said. "Still, you ought to be well in front of Jason."

I checked the stuff with the customs while he put the aircraft away. The official didn't give the mackintosh over my arm a second look.

In a few minutes Maurice joined me and we walked out through the empty echoing halls of what had once been London Airport. A Rolls hire was waiting for us outside. Telling the man to drive us to Boodles Maurice sat back in his seat. "I wired them to keep rooms for us both. Is that all right?" he asked.

"Yes, but I want to be dropped at Eaton Place. That is where Mildred will be—or, at least I hope it is. If I've guessed wrong and Jason has found out right, then we are goosed."

"You don't know where Roddy is?"

"The last I heard of him, he was in search of a pair of trousers some miles south-west of Apt. And the hounds were after him, or at least I imagine they were."

"He'll get through. He has a way of falling on his feet, that young man."

"He is a conceited young pup."

"Don't be too hard on him. He is very young and he has been very successful. You have a way of being too hard on people, Simon, including yourself."

"Perhaps so." I remembered then how he had lifted me off the magnolia and how he had got me out of the smashed Bentley. "He has guts, anyway. So has the girl. I don't suppose I'd be here if it wasn't for them."

He looked at me quickly and then looked away. "Did you know", he said quietly, "that Jason and Sue had something of a walk out, here, earlier in the year?"

"It was all on Jason's side, wasn't it?"

"Perhaps. It's no business of mine, Simon, but that is not what they say. They say it was only the old General who stopped it. He knew Jason's record—his unofficial one that is."

I felt that familiar knot twisting my entrails. Then I remembered her terror of him in Avignon. But I also remembered what she had told me about him when they were together in the château. Perhaps that terror was only transitory. Charm and persistence were the keys to women's hearts and bodies. Just the same I wasn't going to believe it—yet.

"I don't think that can be right," I said in a voice I hardly recognized as my own.

"No. Probably not. But it is what they say. I only mention it because Jason is close behind us. It may, I just say it may, give a personal edge to what he is doing. You humiliated him in the car that time you told me about, remember, and she was there. If he knows Mildred's address, and I suppose he could get it from any of the Dunmanway crowd, you haven't much time. Watch your step."

"I will. Thanks, Maurice. Here we are."

The Rolls purred to a stop in the silent street. I got out. The door swung shut behind me with the satisfactory sonk of hand-built coachwork. I turned back to the car.

"I'll have to go on to Brompton Square after this, Maurice," I said. "I'll ring you."

"Yes, in Boodles. I'll be opening a bottle. Good luck."

The car slid off. There was no other traffic in the street. The tall rows of Victorian houses stared down on me on either side. Except for the parked cars and a man with an umbrella getting into a Lagonda I was quite alone.

The Lady is a Tramp

I walked up the steps under the portico and looked for the name of Miss Evita Manningbury. It was there all right, in very smart lettering on a thin brass plate. I pressed the bell and waited. After a moment or two the door slid silently open in the slightly sinister way such doors have. So somebody was in the flat.

I walked down the narrow hall and commenced to climb the stairs. There was no lift and it was a long climb for Miss Manningbury's flat was the top one. The door was ajar when I got to it. I pushed it open and went into the little hall. The door to the living-room was on the left and somebody was inside. On a record-player in muted tones with the volume turned very low Sinatra was singing "The Lady is a Tramp". I thought it appropriate. I went in.

Mildred was sitting in the armchair almost facing the door. She was alone. A cigarette dangled from her lips and a glass ashtray full of butts was on a table by her elbow. Beside the ashtray was what looked like a man-sized gin and tonic.

She gave a sudden start when she saw me, and a look of something approaching fright crossed her face.

"Simon!" she exclaimed.

"Sorry to disappoint you, my dear," I said. "It seems you were expecting somebody else."

"I certainly wasn't expecting you."

Perhaps it was because I had recently been seeing someone younger and fresher, but when I looked at my wife her appearance was almost frightening. Her face seemed to be falling apart as women's faces do when they are past their first youth and have been on the jag for a week. There were ravages there now which nothing could repair. She had taken, too, to dyeing her hair, and it had been unskilfully done, probably in Dublin. At least had she been

129

living with me my comments would have saved her that degradation. I pondered briefly on how love could change to indifference and then to actual dislike.

There were drinks—bottles of gin and sherry and whisky, tonic and soda and an ice thermos and slices of lemon—on a graceful, tray-topped table beside me. I poured a slug of gin into a heavy cut-glass tumbler, dropped in lemon and ice and sloshed tonic on top of them. It occurred to me as I took up the tumbler that Miss Manningbury liked to have nice things about her. There was an elegant tallboy beside the door, a writing desk in the window which was Hepplewhite or a damn good copy, and an Etty nude over the fireplace. Miss Manningbury, I supposed, would be the sort of girl who liked Etty nudes.

I took the drink and sat in another armchair.

"Make yourself at home," Mildred said.

"Thanks, I rather thought I was."

Mildred exhaled a cloud of tobacco smoke and then, brushing it aside with her hand, leant forward to look at me. "What have you been doing to yourself?" she asked. "You look ten years younger."

It was suddenly brought home to me that I felt ten years younger.

"I suppose you are in that ghastly little bachelor villa of yours?"

"No, not yet. I have been living the simple life, or I suppose you could call it that, and taking a lot of exercise. You should try it sometime."

She took a cigarette from the box beside her and lit it from the stub of her old one. The used one was only half smoked. She crushed it out in the ashtray. Then she picked up her glass, walked over to the drink table and refilled it. Although her face might have gone to hell she had kept her figure and nothing could take away the animal grace with which she moved.

She was giving herself man-sized measures all right, I noticed as she tipped up the gin-bottle. When she had mixed the drink she turned to me with it in her hand. "I'm going to divorce you, Simon," she said harshly. "And if you've heard about it somewhere and have come over to try to make me change my mind you are wasting your time."

"Well," I said. "No, it's not that at all. In fact if you want any assistance I'll be glad to give it to you."

"Then what do you want?"

"An envelope, let's face it. Just a plain, ordinary envelope. It was in a letter addressed to you. You collected it from Mrs. Rogers this morning."

"What has that envelope to do with you?"

"Let's just say it is mine and I want it."

"It isn't yours. What is all this excitement about it, anyway? There are only a lot of figures inside."

I put down my glass. "'All this excitement'?" I said. "Someone else has been looking for it, then?"

"Yes, indeed. You are a little late, Simon."

"Who?"

"Its rightful owner. Roddy Marston. He had a letter from you so of course, dear Simon, I had to give it to him."

"Roddy Marston! How the hell did he get here? Oh well, it doesn't matter now." I hesitated. "You opened the envelope," I said.

"You hardly expected me not to, did you? It sounded all very exciting and intriguing. I must say I was most disappointed."

"No doubt. A set of figures, you said. What sort of figures?"

The Lady is a Tramp

"They were rather like a doctor's prescription."

At that moment the door buzzer sounded in the hall.

"Don't touch that!" I snapped at her as she stretched out her hand. I was too late. She had already pressed the button that freed the lock. Not that it made much difference. It was unlikely that she would have obeyed me. She had never done it before and it was a bit late for starting now.

We waited, looking at each other, while we listened to the footsteps coming up the stairs. Someone was taking the steps two at a time. Someone unhurried yet purposeful, someone who knew what he wanted and was in the way of getting it. I could guess who it was. I had, perhaps, spent rather too much time talking to my wife.

The footsteps reached the head of the stairs and came on down the hall. Then the huge figure of Stuart Jason filled the doorway.

"Come in, Stuart," Mildred said. "I got your wire."

"Old home week," I remarked. "Now we're all a happy family."

Jason bent his head in the way very tall men will in a doorway and came into the room. He wasted no time on the niceties of conversation. "I'm looking for an envelope, Mildred," he said abruptly. "I think you have it. Unless you've given it to him." He jerked his head in my direction.

" 'The bride has departed, the gallant came late—' " I murmured.

"If it's the one with the hieroglyphics on it that everyone seems so interested in, well it's gone," Mildred said. "I gave it to Roddy Marston earlier today."

"Where is he now?" he demanded harshly.

"I wouldn't answer the colonel if I were you," I said.

The Lady is a Tramp

"Until he comes out of the orderly room and into civilization."

He turned directly towards me then. "Get out," he barked.

"What, and leave my dear wife, or ex-wife to be, alone with you? You underestimate my chivalry, Lord Cardigan or is it Redvers Buller? I never can decide which of them was your lineal ancestor—in purely military matters that is to say."

In two strides he was across the room and towering over me. "You're not behind a gun now, Herald," he snapped, his lips drawn in a tight line. "I told you to get out and you're going out."

Taking me by the lapels of my coat he plucked me out of my chair. One of his great hands pinioned my arms behind me. He was immensely strong. I kicked out at him and struggled to get my arms free. It was quite useless. I was like a chicken or a child in his grasp. He carried me across the hall to the stairhead. Then he threw me downstairs.

CHAPTER 9

Hideaway

I think he meant to kill me and he very nearly succeeded. It was the narrowness of the stairs which saved me. I hit first one side wall and then the other and that slowed my rate of descent. I fetched up with a slam in a corner of the landing twenty feet below. As I hit, faintly, far above me, I thought I heard a woman's laugh.

All the breath was knocked out of my body by the brutal shock of the thing, and I had a pretty fair idea that I had broken my back. For some minutes I lay there panting, pain and hate welling up inside me. Then tentatively, and with terror grabbing at my guts, I tried wriggling my toes. They worked.

I got one leg to take my weight and pushed myself up by the wall. I leant there for a bit staring at the door of the second floor flat. The card on it bore the name of a famous film director. I thought it a pity he hadn't seen my performance.

By hanging on to the banisters I got myself downstairs and into the street. Life was beginning to come back to me by then, and I made my way slowly along towards Eaton Terrace. As I went I reflected that the world was rapidly getting too small to hold both Jason and myself.

There was no one in the little pub except a chap in a Brigade of Guards tie arguing with a very smartly dressed blonde. It was something to do with Ascot and the

Enclosure. She kicked him when I came in and he took his voice down a tone or two off Horse Guards Parade. You could still hear him two blocks away. I ordered two double whiskies. When they came I poured one into the other and splashed a little soda on top of them. Even then the drink was only a shade larger than the ordinary Irish double. I told the girl to have another two coming up.

"You all right, dear," she said to me as she served me. "You look a bit shaky."

"So would you if you'd just been thrown downstairs," I said.

The argument about Ascot was cut suddenly short in the middle. I felt rather than saw the pair of them turn and stare at me. The girl behind the bar gave me an old-fashioned look and went away. I finished the first whisky in two gulps and started on the second. It didn't take long to go down either.

"Don't go to Ascot with him," I said to the blonde popsie as I passed. "Come to Le Touquet with me instead. You'll have far more fun."

"That wouldn't be difficult," she said. "When are you leaving?"

The guardsman looked appropriately dumb and horrified as guardsmen do at such moments. I went out into the evening sun and caught a passing cab. The whisky seemed to be doing its job all right.

At Brompton Square an elderly maidservant showed me up to a long narrow drawing-room on the first floor. Sue was sitting in a big sofa in the window, with a book in her hands. Behind and below her I could see the sun on a patch of lawn. Birds sang there; the noise of the traffic was scarcely a hum. It was quiet and peaceful. We might have been in Surrey.

"Hallo," I said. "Any slant-eyed Chinamen disguised as telephone operators been trying to kidnap you lately?" I picked up the book she was reading, and looked at the title. "*W. O. The Autobiography of W. O. Bentley*," I read aloud. "What is this, Sue? Have I made a convert?"

"Did you read it?"

"Yes, it made me want to cry." I put the book down. "Roddy has been back," I said.

"Yes, he——"

Before she could reply a door at the back of the room opened and an old, old man, bent about the shoulders but otherwise very erect, came in. He walked over towards us.

"Uncle," Sue said. "This is Simon Herald."

The old General's eyes were still very bright and piercing under his white eyebrows. I was given a stare from them which seemed to go right through me. "I've heard of you, Herald," he said with a slight smile. "Hannah's. They didn't know what to make of you, did they? Hannah is dead. You knew that?"

"Dead? No, sir. I've been abroad. That must have been quite a funeral."

Susan brought him a glass of sherry and he took it and sipped it. He gave a little sigh. "There are not many of us left now, Herald," he said. "Three major wars and some skirmishes, they thin us out, you know." I remembered that I was in the presence of one of the few still living who had charged at Omdurman with Winston Churchill and who had ridden steeplechases against Fred Withington and Aubrey Hastings. He gave me another of his piercing stares and it made me conscious that in some way I was being sized up. "Private armies," he said. "I forget which one you were in. There were too many of them. They were always a mistake. Winston was too fond of side-shows. Bobs didn't like them; D.H. wouldn't have them at any price. The Duke didn't allow them in the Peninsula. They were right; swashbucklers make bad soldiers." He put down his glass. "My niece and nephew are up to something, Herald," he said directly. "I don't know what it is for they tell me very little. They need a hand on the reins. I hope you can supply it." Then he walked out of the room.

When the door shut I turned to her again. "How the devil did your brother get to Mildred before me?" I asked.

She laughed. "By using something you say he hasn't got," she said.

"What's that?"

"His brains. He rang Hector Dunmanway from Paris to ask him where your wife was. Hector told him she was on her way to London and gave him her address. He flew over and was on the doorstep waiting for her."

"Where is he now?"

"He has gone back to France or is on his way there. He wouldn't tell me how he was going to travel. He said he was going to contact Legarde—that's the head of the American syndicate—somehow. And, Simon, he realizes now that he can't take on these people by himself. He wants your help—if you'll give it to him."

"He's going to get it whether he wants it or not," I said, grimly, remembering Jason. "What does he want me to do?"

"He left me Legarde's address. Here it is."

I took the slip of paper she handed me. *Villa Simone, Mont Boron, Nice,* was written on it.

"Yes?" I said.

"Could you see Legarde and tell him that Roddy is still in the market?"

"That's easy. What then?"

"If you can leave a message with Legarde where Roddy can meet you he'll manage to do it somehow. Then the two of you can think up a way of getting the formula to him."

"I suppose that is as good an idea as any. And if I see Legarde I might be able to fix up a meeting place there and then which he can convey to your brother."

"You'll do it?"

"I'll do it all right," I said grimly. "Don't worry about that. But I'll have to think of a way of getting to France. They seem to have the airlines pretty well covered. But, by Jove, Maurice said something about going back to keep an eye on the building. I'll ring him now."

"Simon," she said quietly. "I'm coming with you."

"Don't be a fool, Sue. Of course you're not."

"I've talked it over with Roddy and it is the only way. Can't you see—if I stay here they can do exactly what they did before. And I'll be terrified every time I set foot outside the door. It will make nonsense of everything you and Roddy try to do. You'll have to take me with you, Simon."

"Haven't you a maiden aunt somewhere you can go and stay with?"

"No, and even if I had it wouldn't be fair to her. They'd be certain to find us out."

"But this is ridiculous——"

"Perhaps, but I'm coming just the same." Her chin had a determined tilt to it which I had seen before. I didn't deny that it made life brighter that she wanted to be with me, that the thought of having her there was payment itself for the task I was taking on. Then I remembered about what Maurice had said concerning Jason and her. I

opened my mouth to speak and then shut it again. It was
hardly the time to bring up the subject. I felt no desire to
disclose that my rival—if he was such—had just thrown
me downstairs.

There was a telephone on a table near the door. I walked
over, picked up the receiver and dialled Boodles' number.
Maurice was there and after a little while he came to the
box.

"Maurice," I said. "How soon are you going back to
France?"

"I've got a few things to do here. I want to see my
stockbroker, though I don't suppose that will do me much
good, and one or two other bits of business. I suppose the
end of the week."

"You couldn't by any chance make it earlier? Tomorrow, for instance? That matter I told you about has
been boiling up again."

"Yes, Simon, I could, if it helps you along."

"Thanks, Maurice. I thought you would. There'll be
an extra passenger. Sue is coming."

There was the faintest hesitation at the other end of the
phone. Then he said: "I saw a mutual friend in the club
just now. Did he catch up with you?"

"Yes," I said grimly. "He did, Maurice. That is one of
the reasons I am going back to France."

We took off from Croydon early next morning, checked
customs at Le Touquet and had an uneventful flight down
the Rhône Valley and along the coast. This time, Maurice
said, he had decided to make his headquarters in St.
Tropez. He wanted to keep a closer eye on how the work
on the villa was going, so we landed at Fréjus amongst the
helicopters and the army aircraft instead of at Mandelieu.
As usual he had everything laid on and a car was waiting

for him. I phoned St. Raphael for a taxi to come and collect us. When it came we said good-bye to Maurice and I told the driver to take us to Cannes.

There was no doubt in my mind where we were going. I knew of only one place which came near to being a safe refuge. It was my cottage which was tucked into a fold in the hills above Cannes. There, I thought, I would leave Sue whilst I sought out Legarde. Madame Huron and her husband would look after her and she would be as safe there as anywhere. I had told Maurice where we were going, and he had promised to get in touch with me should he hear anything which might be useful.

The narrow dirt road crawling upwards to the cottage was just as I remembered it. So was the cottage itself. It was a tiny white affair with a red tiled roof and bougainvillea spilling all over it. There were two bedrooms, a couple of bathrooms, a kitchen and a living-room. The living-room ran along the front of the house; french windows opened on to a flagged terrace and gave a view of the hills and the sea.

The cottage was indeed a relic of my bachelor days. Mildred had seen it once and had hated it. It was much too far from what she called civilization. Mildred's excursions to the south of France did not take her far from the Croisette, and she did not much care for the French people who required to be spoken to in their own language.

The Hurons had kept their promise to look after it for me, the flower beds had been tended and watered, the tiles in the little crescent-shaped pool under the mimosa tree were clean and sparkling. They had got my wire too, for the pool was filling and the door and windows stood open.

I should want the driver again, to take me to pick up the Bentley, so I told him to wait. Then I went down the slope to the Hurons' house. It was surrounded by a patch of vines and lay about a hundred yards below the cottage.

Madame Huron came to meet me. She was a woman of about fifty on whom a lifetime of hard work had left its mark. She looked quite twenty years older than she was. Her face was worn and wrinkled and wisps of grey hair wound about the sides of her head. She wore a faded, shapeless dress and kindness was written all over her.

"Ah, M'sieu, M'sieu," she said when she saw me. "You have come back. Jacques!" she called. "Jacques! *C'est M'sieu Herald.*"

Her husband came round the corner of the house, doffing his blue cap as he came, a smile of welcome on his grizzled face. "You are older, M'sieu," he said to me as he took my hand.

"It touches all of us, *mon vieux*," I replied.

I saw them looking past me and I turned. Sue was coming down the slope towards us. She was smiling. They looked at me and they looked at her. Their faces lit up and they smiled too.

"This is Mademoiselle Marston," I said to them. "I shall perhaps be away for a little while and I want you to look after her."

"*Volontiers*, M'sieu," they said. "We shall take good care of her."

After talking for a few moments with them we walked back to the cottage. There was a Provençal dresser in the living-room where we kept most of the household things. I showed her this and the rest of the house. It didn't take much showing but I noticed again how everything had been prepared for us and how spotless the house was.

"It's enchanting, Simon," she said. "How did you ever come to find it?"

Hideaway

"I bought it from one of those English *émigrés* who used to swarm around this coast before the war. Taxation has killed almost all of them off now. This chap had a big estate in the mountains. He built this cottage for a *chère amie* but she left him almost as soon as it was finished. I came on him just when he wanted to get rid of it."

"Did—did Mildred ever come here?"

"Once. She looked at it, hated it and went straight back to the Carlton." I picked up the mackintosh I had carried so carefully with me from London, and put my hand into its pocket. "I'm going now," I said. "I'll collect the Bentley and make contact with Legarde. Just in case anything should happen I'm leaving you this." I took out the revolver.

She looked at it lying in my hand. "But, Simon, I haven't the faintest idea how to use it."

"Nor have ninety per cent of the people who try to. It's a deterrent more than anything else. But if you have to, point it, pull the trigger and pray. That should be enough."

"Don't you want it yourself?"

"No, and I don't think you will either, but I'd feel happier if you had it." I took six of the short stubby cartridges and pushed them home. Then I handed her the gun. "Keep it beside you," I said. "It will give you confidence, anyway."

She took it from me, weighed it in her hand and dropped it into the wide pocket of her skirt. "It's surprisingly light," she said.

"It's supposed to be the best balanced of them all."

She looked at its outline in her pocket. "Calamity Jane, my hat!" she said. "You do think up the strangest things, Simon, and it's nice of you to leave it. But can't I come too?"

"No. I'm sorry, Sue. You're safer here. I'll get in touch with you as soon as I can."

For every reason in the world I hated to leave her. She wanted me to stay; it was written all over her. Yet I knew that if I stayed I might stay too long. And, besides, somehow I always seemed to see the spectre of Stuart Jason standing between us. That was something I had to get sorted out later on.

I walked out to the car and told the driver to take me to Nice. As we went down the road I turned and looked back. She was standing in the doorway, a slim figure in white. She raised an arm, waved, and then went back to the cottage.

CHAPTER 10

Checkmate

The Bentley was where I had left her, in the car park of the airport. I drove through Nice, round the port and turned to the left off the Lower Corniche. I thought that Sue was safe enough. It was unlikely that they were hunting for us. It was Roddy whom they would be after for they would of course now know that he had reclaimed the envelope from Mildred. The trouble was that Mildred did know of the existence of the cottage and Jason knew Mildred as indeed everyone knew everyone else in the society in which I moved. I worried about it a bit as I climbed up through the forest, and then came to the conclusion that I was fussing unnecessarily. There was no reason in the world why they should be interested in us any more. But I thought I should get back to the cottage as soon as I could.

I left the car in the car park on the plateau and went into the café that looks down on to Cap Ferrat.

There weren't many people about and the waiter who brought me my St. Raphael was disposed to gossip. In no time at all I had learnt where M'sieu Legarde, the American millionaire, lived. In fact, it was so near he came to the entrance and pointed it out to me.

It was about five hundred yards down from the summit on the left-hand side of the road. There was an archway over the gate and a drive going down at a steep angle. The 'house itself was a substantial one, two storeys high with a steep-pitched roof. It was covered with creeper and looked much older than most of the houses in the locality. The cicadas were clacking all about me as I walked down the drive. Apart from them it was very quiet, and it was very hot.

The door was open but inside it was a mosquito screen stretching from wall to wall. Through the screen I could see into two long, cool-looking rooms full of heavy furniture which opened out on either side of a wide hall. There were rugs on the tiles of the hall and at the far end a graceful, curving stone staircase led upwards.

An old-fashioned bell-pull was let into the jamb of the door. I gave it a tug and heard the sound of a bell ringing somewhere in the depths of the house.

No one came. After a bit I gave the bell another, stronger pull. This time the noise was more distinct and went on longer. The bell was working, anyway. Still no one came.

When the bell stopped ringing I listened attentively but there was no sound of life in the house at all. I could see pretty well the whole of the room on either side of the hall and there was no one there. Putting out my hand I gave the mosquito screen a shove. It swung silently open. I stepped inside.

There were ornately carved oak chairs and cupboards and some stiff-looking settees in the downstairs rooms and each of them had huge, Mexican fireplaces and overmantels. The windows had mosquito screens over them and the heavy leaves of the creeper helped to shut out the light. The whole effect was depressing.

There was no one about. I didn't want to go until I had at least tried to make contact with the man or found somewhere to leave a note or a message for him. The stairs looked the next best bet. I went up them.

At the top, on the left, was a little gallery. The outer wall of this was one huge window. There was light here all right. The window gave a view down over the vineyards to Villefranche and Cap Ferrat, and, further away, you could see the whole sweep of the hills to where Eze was perched on its pinnacle. In front of the window was a long, deep sofa; a refectory table with a telephone on it took up most of the rest of the floor space. The wall facing the window was one huge built-in bookcase. This was filled, so far as I could see, with novels of the nineteen twenties in their dust-jackets. Huxley and Firbank and Hemingway, and Edgar Wallace, Sapper and Warwick Deeping for good measure, were all there; below them were a couple of shelves of elaborately bound *erotica*. Mr. Legarde appeared to have a strange taste in literature as well as in furniture. I was certainly meeting interesting people, or should be if I could find anyone.

At the end of the gallery an archway led into another room in the front of the house. It had been fitted up as a rather ghastly games' room, with a bar, a billiard table, a juke-box, a dart-board and a few easy chairs for drinking in. On the walls were murals which looked as if they might have been copied from the illustrations in the books in the lower shelves outside. There were two tall windows from which the creeper had been cut back and through them I could see the drive and the gateway. But this room, too, was empty.

As I hesitated which way to turn the telephone on the refectory table suddenly started to ring.

I walked back through the archway and looked at it. Well, this might tell me something, I thought. I picked up the receiver.

Checkmate

There was a click as the connection was made and then the inevitable pause. I sat down on the end of the sofa to take the call. From where I sat I could see straight out through the windows to the gateway. As I looked a car, a big buff Mercedes, slid to a stop across the entrance, blocking it. Two men got out of the back in a hurry and slammed the doors. They started down the drive. I recognized one of them.

"Is that you, Legarde?" said a voice in my ear. It was distorted and crackling as voices usually are over French telephones but I had no trouble at all in knowing whose it was. Roddy Marston was at the other end of the telephone.

"No, it is not," I said. "It's Herald, and I think I've walked into trouble. I haven't much time so listen while I tell you what to do. Go to my cottage. . . ." Quickly I gave him directions for getting there.

"What sort of trouble are you in?" he asked as I finished.

"I don't know but I've a feeling I'll pretty soon find out. Ring off and get going. I'll join you when I can." I put down the receiver.

Stuart Jason came round the head of the stairs and faced me. He had the big Webley in his hand. It was pointed straight at my chest. The muzzle looked the size of a cannon.

CHAPTER 11

A Glass of Wine at Cap Ferrat

The Webley was cocked and the hand that held it was as steady as a vice. Even if he was a lousy shot, and I had no evidence that he was, at that distance he could scarcely miss. I knew well enough what those big slugs could do to you at short range. I was on the wrong side of the gun this time. Now it was his finger which was in front of the trigger. Very slowly and carefully I brought up my hands and placed them flat, palm downwards, on the table in front of me.

"Who were you talking to on the telephone?" he asked. That, anyway, was a relief. He had not heard what I had been saying.

"Legarde's wine merchant," I said. "He was ringing for his weekly order."

"You don't expect me to believe that?"

"No. Not particularly."

"Where is Marston?"

"I don't know. I've parted with that young man."

"Maybe we can persuade you to tell us. Stand up."

I obeyed. There didn't seem much point in doing anything else.

"Now walk to the stairs and go down them."

He wasn't taking any chances. I suppose, in a way, it was a sort of compliment. His eyes never left me for a moment. When I passed him on the way to the stairhead he stepped backwards so that I should not have an opportunity of jumping him. The revolver never left its point of aim which was my navel or as near it as makes no matter. He needn't have worried. I didn't want one of those big slugs in my stomach. I was not going to try anything until the odds came a bit my way again.

"You can put that Buntline Special up," I said. "I'll go quietly."

A sallow-complexioned man who looked, and I suppose was, a Sicilian pistoleer, was waiting at the bottom of the stairs. He leant forward as I came within his reach and patted me from my shoulders to my hips. "O.K.," he said. "He's clean."

"Take off his coat and turn out his pockets," Jason ordered.

"I prefer to do my own undressing," I said. I got out of the coat and handed it to him. He felt it all over and spilled the contents of its pockets on to a small table.

"Nothing here," he said.

"We've got one of them, anyway." Jason appeared to hesitate. Then he said, "Take him along. I want to telephone."

The pistoleer threw my coat back to me. Then he took a Lüger from under his left armpit and motioned towards the door. I walked in front of him to the car. Veletti was behind the wheel. He did not look at me but sat staring out through the windscreen. I was pushed into the back and the pistoleer got in beside me. After a minute or two Jason came out from the house and got into the front seat beside Veletti. The car pulled off.

We went straight on across the plateau, over the top of Mont Boron and down the steep, ramp-like road that leads to the Moyen Corniche. Here Veletti turned sharply right-handed and into the narrow winding descent to Villefranche. He was going at a great pace and it occurred to me to wonder what would happen if we met anyone coming up. This, also, apparently occurred to Jason. "Not so fast, damn you. Not so damn fast," he growled.

Veletti slowed a trifle, but not much. We reached the Lower Corniche without incident and took the turn for Cap Ferrat. After about a mile we turned through ornate gates and started to ascend a steeply climbing drive. This must, I supposed, lead to Mantovelli's residence which, judging by the way we were climbing, must lie on the very spine of the Cap. Then the car stopped, the pistoleer prodded me with the muzzle of his gun and I got out.

We had come to a halt in front of the porch of a huge nineteenth-century villa. There were turrets, and dormer windows and things that looked like the tops of pagodas all over the place. Three steps led up to a glass-covered porch. From this swinging glass doors gave into the interior of the house. Outside these doors a youngish man in horn-rimmed glasses with a sheaf of papers under his arm was waiting for us.

"Good afternoon, Mr. Herald," he said to me. "M. Mantovelli is most anxious to see you. Will you come along with me, please?"

We went into the house. There was a rectangular stone hallway or patio which seemed to take up the entire centre of the building. Galleries ran around its sides and from these tapestries hung. It was cool in here especially after the heat and the glare outside. I was brought to a staircase which climbed up through a tower on the left of the entrance, and then down one side of the gallery overlooking the hall.

"You wouldn't remember me, of course," my escort

said, "but we met years ago at Oxford. In your cousin's rooms. You had just come back from Shelsey Walsh."

"Oh, yes," I said politely, wondering how many more of Mantovelli's young men were going to claim acquaintance with me.

"It was just before the war. You were driving then, I think?"

"I had just started," I remembered my very maiden effort at Shelsey in a second-hand special.

"How do you think the pre-war drivers compare with those today? Birkin and Brooks, Moss and Seaman, that sort of thing?"

"I only saw Birkin once and I was a schoolboy then. The Bentley boys were a good deal older than the chaps driving today. I don't know whether that makes much difference. I would say that with the exception of Seaman, whom you have just mentioned, all the pre-war British drivers were amateurs and the present-day drivers are professionals. That is your answer, really, isn't it? But you must realize that I'm not at all competent to judge. I never got within kicking distance of that class."

"Oh, surely you do yourself an injustice there. I read your press-cuttings, you know. As a matter of fact I was in charge of getting them. We were wondering, M. Mantovelli and I, why you gave up. It was one of the questions about you which bothered us, you know. Ah, here we are."

A waist-high, iron grille ran across the entrance to a loggia which was open in front to the weather. Inside were some gilt armchairs upholstered in silk and a gilt-legged table with a marble top. On the table was a tray bearing a teapot and a tiny cup and saucer. With his back to us in one of the chairs a man was sitting. There was no mistaking that leathery neck nor the square set of the shoulders in the very straight-cut suit. It was Mantovelli and I wondered what he had to say to me.

My companion opened a gate in the grille. "Mr. Herald is here now, sir," he said.

The millionaire did not move or turn his head. His dry, crackling voice came over his shoulder. "Sit down, Herald," he said. "I want to talk to you."

I pulled up a chair on the side of the table opposite to him. Behind me I heard the gate in the grille open. A manservant in a white coat came in carrying a tray. On it were a bottle of champagne in a wine cooler and a thin, fluted glass. He poured the wine into the glass, put the bottle back into the cooler and went away. There was a gold swizzle stick on the tray beside the glass. I picked it up and dunked it in the wine. Then I lifted the glass to my lips and sipped. It was superb. "Very nice," I said, putting down the glass. "This, I suppose, is to put the charm into captivity. What do you want with me, Mantovelli?"

He did not answer for a moment but sat there, his chin on his chest, his leathery, saurian cheeks seamed and wrinkled, his old eyes deep in their cavernous sockets, gazing out at the formal garden below us. It was worth looking at. Two cropped and cared-for lawns were divided by an ornamental canal. Where the lawns ended was a small, rocky cliff. Down this cliff, between a row of cypresses, an artificial waterfall came cascading. A tiny Palladian temple was perched on the top of the cliff. Beyond and below the sun sparkled on the sea and the whole curve of the coast to Cannes lay before our eyes in a gaudy haze of blue.

"Herald," he said at length, without looking at me, "how would you like to work for me?"

A Glass of Wine at Cap Ferrat

I sat up in my chair. He did not move his head but he stretched out his hand towards the table. With the gold-headed stick still dangling from his little finger he lifted the cup of tea to his lips.

"Before I answer," I said, "there is something I want to know. Why was Legarde's house empty and why did you go to all this trouble to bring me here? I take it it wasn't just to offer me a job?"

"Not entirely. Legarde and I are interested in acquiring the same thing. Legarde wishes to obtain it by purchase and I am prepared to use other means when purchase fails. I came to an arrangement with Legarde by which, shall I say, I bought out his interest. Also he was kind enough to allow me the use of his house for a day or two. We both expected that the house would receive a visitor within that time and a watch was set. Unfortunately one Englishman looks very like another and the trap was sprung on the wrong man. Still, I have been wanting to have a talk with you for some little time. Now, what is the answer to my offer?"

"The answer is no," I said firmly.

He sighed and lifted the cup to his lips again. "That is a pity," he said. Then, after a pause. "Why did you give up motor-racing?" he asked.

There didn't seem much point in beating about the bush. In a way it was a relief to say it to someone. "I was frightened," I said.

He looked at me with a sudden flash of interest in his cold eyes.

"I guessed so," he said. "You are candid, Herald. I believe you to be an intelligent man. You have shown that you can fight and think. The life that I am offering you would be congenial. My young men like it."

"I daresay. But I don't much care for your led-captain."

"Nor he for you. But your paths need not cross."

"What premium am I expected to put up as the price of this splendid appointment?"

His voice was suddenly harsh. "I want to know young Marston's whereabouts," he said.

"Then I am afraid that the price is too high."

He sighed again. His sudden anger seemed to have passed. "I am an old man, Herald," he said. "I am told that my life is hanging by a thread. I believe that when that thread snaps there is nothing more. I believe that we have here on earth all we are going to get; henceforward is oblivion. And I have lived on that assumption. I regret nothing I have done. Why should I? The objectives which I have set myself I have so far succeeded in attaining. If lesser men have had to be swept aside it was their misfortune for standing in my way. I do not intend to be baulked now. Do I make myself clear?"

"Perfectly." I could guess what was coming. The sun was like a sheet of warmth outside. It was cool in the loggia but not cool enough to explain the chill that was creeping across my back as the hard, dry old voice crackled on.

"I have only one ambition which as yet remains to be fulfilled. My doctor, you must meet him, perhaps you will have to, tells me that the hope of attaining it is the only thing which is keeping me alive. I intend to fulfil that ambition, Herald, and neither you nor Marston nor any other whippersnapper, nor that girl in whom you have recently been displaying an interest, is going to stand in my way. You have held me up too long already. You have made a fool of Jason and damaged his prestige. You have done very well in a short time and with the resources at your disposal, but you have run your course. Once more,

Herald, and this is for the last time, is it peace or war?"

"War," I said.

"Very well. You leave me no option. I am handing you over to Colonel Jason." He stretched out his hand towards a bell beside the tray.

I took the bottle of champagne from the cooler and re-filled my glass. "Tell him to wait until I have finished this wine," I said. "It is quite extraordinarily good."

He looked at me face to face then and his dry crackling laugh came up from somewhere inside him. "It is a pity you could not accept my offer," he said. "We would have got on together."

That, at least, was true; for I had to admit that in some extraordinary way I liked the old man. He was a robber baron born out of his time and yet twisting the time to his own ends. He was ruthless, anti-social, amoral, and anything else you liked to call him, yet he had in him an astringent acceptance of facts and a sense of the humour in things with which I found myself in sympathy. After all I hadn't much use for accepted taboos myself. At least part of me would have enjoyed working for him and enjoyed it very much. Also, I was frightened. I wondered if he knew how much it had cost me to refuse his offer.

Taking the glass in my hand I stood up and walked to the edge of the loggia.

"You cannot get out that way," said his voice behind me with a hint of amusement in it. "The drop is much too high."

"I thought it would be," I answered. "Still, it was worth trying."

Faintly I could hear the splash of the waterfall. One of the household in white flannels reclined in a lounging chair in the shade, reading a novel. Somewhere I thought I heard a woman's laugh. It was all very peaceful. For everyone, that is to say, except for me.

As I turned away from the view I considered whether it would be worthwhile offering violence to the old man. Perhaps I could hold him hostage for my freedom. . . .

He read my thoughts like an open book. "If you are contemplating physical assault," he said, "I would not advise that course." He gave a faint nod of his head. Behind him, in the shadows beyond the grille, I saw a movement. A guard was stationed there. So that course was out. I turned to look at the pictures on the walls, my mind racing desperately.

"Fragonards," he said. "You admired my Cézannes. You like these pretties, too?"

"Charming," I said. "But just at the moment they hardly fit in with my mood."

"You may as well tell us where Marston is. We shall find out anyway. It will save you a lot of, well, inconvenience."

"No."

"Very well. It is time." He touched the bell.

The pistoleer came from the shadows at the back. He beckoned and I left the loggia. As we walked away I turned to look behind me.

Mantovelli was still sitting, immovable, his head sunk on his chest, staring out at the little waterfall and the Palladian temple above it. What his thoughts were I did not know. I was pretty sure pity was not amongst them.

We went back along the gallery, past the tapestries and the paintings and the priceless furniture and all the rest of the loot acquired by a lifetime of plunder and pillage. There was movement now in the great square hall. Jason was stalking about barking orders and various people were running to obey.

A Glass of Wine at Cap Ferrat

Through the glass windows of the curving staircase I saw the triangular sails of yachts outlined against the blue of the sea and the mountains. Somewhere, I supposed, some people were enjoying themselves on this sun-swept coast. I was not one of them.

The huge thug whom I had left trussed up in the foothills of the Luberons was standing at the bottom of the staircase. Sue need not have worried. Someone had found him, all right. I heartily wished they had not. Jason was a few feet behind him.

"All right, Beppo," Jason said to the thug. "He is yours from now on."

Beppo looked at me and grinned. It was not a friendly grin. By and large, I remembered, Beppo would have quite a score to settle with me. I walked out in front of them into the sun.

The buff Mercedes was drawn up just beyond the steps with a driver whom I did not recognize at the wheel. Beppo opened one of the back doors. His great hand gripped my shoulder, twisted it and sent me spinning into the car. He got in after me and pushed me casually across the seat so that I fetched up with a bang in the corner. Jason sat beside the driver. We went down the long drive and out on to the main highway of the Cap.

No attempt was made to conceal me. To the casual observer we were merely four peaceful people in a car proceeding at a high speed which, heaven knows, is not unusual in France, from one place to another. The insolence of it annoyed me but there was very little that I could do about it. Beppo sat very close to me, almost crushing me. He looked at me with an evil and anticipatory grin on his face as if to ask me to try something on. I didn't.

At the entrance to Cap Ferrat instead of turning on to

A Glass of Wine at Cap Ferrat

the Corniche, as I expected, we went down into Ville-franche. In a few moments we were pulling up on the quay-side. Beppo hooked his arm through mine and yanked me out of the car. Before I quite knew what was happening I was in a motor-boat which was moving across Villefranche harbour.

A long, graceful yacht was lying at anchor about a hundred yards away. I knew now where we were going. As we came around her stern I read the name in gilt letters against the white of her hull. *La Paloma*. This was Manto-velli's fabulous craft on which in his younger days he had thrown the most sought after parties of the Coast. And those were the days when the Coast really was the centre of the *haut monde* and café society, when the campers had not come and the rival attractions of Jamaica and the West Indian Islands had not drawn off the cream of the rich, the beautiful and the damned.

We came alongside and at a nod from Jason Beppo brought me on to the deck, down a companionway and into a cabin.

It was fitted up as a stateroom with a bed, a wardrobe and a writing desk. There was a thick carpet and some chairs and the whole thing would have done credit to a transatlantic liner. But the two huge men, Jason and Beppo, seemed to fill it and to leave no room for anything else. The sensation of being confined into a small space with these two grim silent giants, both of whom had reason to hate me, was terrifying.

This was it. No one knew where I was. There was no likelihood of my trail being picked up. I could guess very accurately what was about to happen. Roddy Marston's whereabouts were going to be beaten and tortured out of me. Had they picked me up three hours ago, except for the physical agony, they could have done nothing to me for I did not know where Marston was. But now I did, for I myself had told him on the telephone to go to the cottage. In all probability he was there now. And so was Sue.

At the thought of her I almost groaned aloud. I was no hero and I knew it. I wondered how much of this I was going to be able to stand and for how long. These people were experts. Jason had earned his reputation for sadism and beatings-up during the war and presumably he had had plenty of practice since in Mantovelli's service. Beppo would take pleasure in taking out my sinews at his direction. Afterwards, I supposed, they would kill me. That would be easy, too. A well-weighted corpse would be slipped overboard from *La Paloma* one night. No one nowadays really bothered about the disappearance of another Englishman abroad, especially if Mantovelli's money was buying silence.

All I could do was to hang on as best I could and not to let them see my terror.

The two of them stood, side by side, looking down at me. I stared back at them.

"Where is Marston?" Jason asked.

"I don't know."

Jason nodded. Beppo's huge fist came up slowly. In the confined space of the cabin I could do nothing to avoid it. It took me on the side of the head and slammed me against the wall.

"Who were you talking to on the telephone?"

"I've told you. Legarde's wine merchant."

"Don't be a fool."

This time the fist took me on the other side of the face. I fell sideways on to one of the chairs, half knocked out, my head singing.

Beppo bent over me. From behind him he took a length of thin, tough cord. With this he lashed me to the chair. He knew what he was doing and he made the cords bite into my flesh. The pain was agonizing and it cleared my head. There was something peculiar about the way he tied me up and it bothered me. Both my arms were securely lashed to the back of the chair so it had nothing to do with them. Then I looked down. They had left my right leg, the one I had broken at Le Mans, the one which was five-eighths of an inch shorter than it should have been, free and untethered.

"Now listen to me," Jason commanded. "You are going to tell us where young Marston is."

"Go to hell," I said. It was not of the highest standards of repartee but it would have to do for the moment.

"Beppo wants to leave you something to remember him by, don't you, Beppo?"

Beppo nodded twice, grinned and nodded again. Then I realized something. The great brute was dumb.

"Show him then," Jason said.

The huge hands felt down my thigh until, unerringly, they came to the place just above the mended break. His mouth opened in a grin. I thought I was going to scream.

Leaving one hand at the break the giant reached down and gripped my foot. Slowly he began to bring it up, pressing his huge weight on my thigh as he did so.

"Of course," Jason remarked conversationally, "other parts of the leg may go first. The knee, for instance. In fact it almost certainly will. Then your leg will not be much use to you at all, will it? I don't think there will be much left to walk on whatever happens."

"Damn you," I said through clenched teeth. I could feel sinew and muscle taking the strain. Soon the bone would have it and then, presumably something was going to go. I clamped my teeth together, hard, and set myself to stick it—if I could. The pain became excruciating.

"All right, Beppo," Jason's voice suddenly cut in.

The great hands fell away and my leg dropped down, limp and aching beside the chair.

"That is a taste of what is going to happen to you," Jason said to me. "I'm giving you half an hour to think it over. Be quite sure we shall have it out of you one way or another. You won't be much good for anything, ever again, unless you talk."

"How the hell can I tell you what I don't know?" I said.

"That is what I intend to find out—in half an hour. There is a clock on the wall."

They left the cabin and the door swung shut behind them.

I sat there, roped to the chair, sick with fear. My leg and my arms were hurting like hell. My eyes were on the minute hand of the clock. It was at ten minutes past the hour, I remember, and it suddenly, or so it seemed, began to move very fast indeed.

Looking back on it my fear was, I think, as much for what I should do, how I should behave under the torture which was coming, as for the actual pain itself. I had failed before. I had given up driving when, or so I had always told myself, with a little more guts I might have gone on. The knowledge and reminder of those grim days of trial and funk and fear were seldom absent from my mind. Now I was desperately afraid that I was going to crack again.

Then, too, they had unerringly found my weakest spot, or Mantovelli had for I doubted if Jason had the brains to think it up for himself. Anyone who has had a badly broken limb knows the dread of another break in the same place. That dread was with me now, together with the memory of the days and nights of pain that I had endured from the original break.

A little later another, more insidious, thought came to me. Why not tell them, it said, just as Jason had suggested? Sooner or later I was sure to crack under the torture just as better men than I had done before. Why not tell them then first rather than last and save myself the pain and the agony, for, if I cracked, then that pain and agony were all for nothing. Why not? Well, the best of all reasons why not was that I could not go on living with myself if I did, but then I had lived with myself for ten years after I had run away from racing. So why not? They would be back in twenty minutes. God it was nearer fifteen, now!

I tugged my glance away from the clock. As I did so I saw the handle of the door begin to turn. Very slowly the door was pushed open. One of them, Beppo no doubt, was coming back before his time.

CHAPTER 12

Le Crépuscule des Dieux

The door opened until there was a gap of a foot or so between it and the jamb. Then it stopped. I felt my heart begin to bang about with a sort of mad, improbable hope. Whoever was outside it could scarcely be either Beppo or Jason, for they would not have concerned themselves with these stealthy precautions but would have come straight on in.

A slim figure slid through the opening, pushed the door gently to, and stood with his back to it.

"Toni Veletti!" I gasped. "What——"

He was across to me in two strides. "Quiet," he whispered in my ear. "I'll explain afterwards."

I heard the click of a clasp knife opening. Then I felt the blade working at my bonds. The ends fell away from my wrists and in a moment or so I was free. I stretched my limbs, feeling the numbness in them and the tingling and the pain as the blood started to flow again.

"There is a motor-boat moored alongside," Toni said softly. "It is a small boat with a tarpaulin in the stern. Go now, quickly. No one is about. Hide under the tarpaulin." Then he was gone.

I went to the door and opened it. There was absolute silence save for a radio playing somewhere, far away. I shut the door behind me. Then, hugging the wall, I made for the companionway. The silence persisted; nobody came along. The deck was empty. Two minutes later I was under the tarpaulin. It was heavy and dirty and stank of fish. Stuffy and noisome as it was I was never so glad to be anywhere in my life.

Steps came down the ship's ladder and someone jumped lightly into the boat. A hand reached over the tarpaulin, brushing me. There was a tug at the outboard engine and then another; it coughed, fired and picked up and we chugged away.

After a minute or two Toni spoke. "I'm going to land you on the rocks behind Mont Boron," he said. "There isn't much time, so you must jump for it. When I say 'now' come out from under there and go. I want to speak to you, Simon. When you get ashore go to the Opera House. Box 9. I shall be there, waiting for you. Are you ready—Now!"

He twitched aside the canvas sheet. I stood up, steadying myself against the sway of the boat. The rocks were a dark mass in front of me. I put my foot on the gunwale and jumped.

They were rough and slippery. I came down with a crash, taking most of the skin off my legs. I didn't care. I was away from the yacht and out of the clutches of Jason and Beppo. I would have cheerfully jumped off the Clifton Suspension Bridge if Toni had told me to. As I picked myself up I saw the little boat chug off into the night with a wake of phosphorescence spreading out behind her.

I clambered over the rocks and made my way to the steps up from the bathing place. When I had climbed them I was on the steep sloping road that leads down from the approach to Mont Boron. I could not for the life of me imagine what Toni was up to. However, the next hour would reveal that, I supposed, and the least I owed him was to keep the rendezvous. What I wanted to do was to get the Bentley and beat it straight back to the cottage. I sat down on the wall at the side of the road for a minute or two, getting my breath back and trying to think things out.

In the end I decided to go up to Mont Boron and collect the Bentley, if it was still there. I would then drive down to the Opera House in it and thus have something to escape by if I was sticking my head into another of Mantovelli's machinations.

It was a long and heavy walk up the hill and through the forest. When I got near Legarde's house I left the road and made a wide detour. It might still be watched for all I knew and I wasn't taking any more chances than I had to that night. I stumbled on a good lot of uninhibited love which was lying about and got pretty well cursed for it. One angry chap accused me of being a *voyeur* and only the most abject of apologies persuaded him that I wasn't. I must say I felt that I had had enough physical violence just then without being assaulted by an interrupted enthusiast.

Nobody had bothered about the Bentley; it was sitting quite safely and majestically amongst the other parked cars. I took the route Veletti had followed a few hours before but I turned to the left at the bottom of the hill leaving Mont Boron. A moon was coming up; the whole of the Baie des Anges and the great hollow in the hills in which Nice is built lay illuminated below me. There was not much traffic about and the big car dropped me fast and silently down into the city. I parked as near to the Opera House as I could and then made my way along to it.

The narrow hall was empty save for a couple of attendants and a gendarme very spick and span in his white gauntlets and equipment. I went up the stairs and then, keeping an eye out for possible trouble, walked behind the boxes looking for Number 9. When I found it I rapped gently on the door. Toni's voice called me to come in.

The crash of the music hit me as soon as I opened the door. It was Wagner with all the stops out. Toni was alone. His chin on his hand, rapt, intent, he sat in the front of the box looking towards the stage. Without turning round he motioned me to a chair behind him. Pulling it well into the shadows at the back of the box I sat down. At least I should be safely hidden here, and I was glad enough to be able to let my muscles relax for a little. But Wagner is, to put it mildly, not a restful composer. I did not know enough about his works to recognize which one was being performed but, whatever it was, it rolled out in great waves of sound, crashing against the tiers of boxes, drumming up to the roof and filling the whole auditorium with its vibrant thunder. Sterling stuff, no doubt, but I was scarcely in the mood for it.

An elaborate programme, cream-coloured, embossed and decked in gilt, lay beside Toni on the front of the box. Leaning forward I picked it up. *Le Crépuscule des Dieux*, I read. The Twilight of the Gods. Well, perhaps that was appropriate enough. I turned over the pages and then put the programme down again and looked once more at Toni. He was still lost, still in his own particular Nirvana, still drinking it in.

At last it ceased. The lights went up and the boxes opposite began to empty as people filed out for the interval. It seemed to me like calm after a storm but then I never have been a great lover of Wagner.

Toni turned to me with a smile. "Now we can talk," he said. "You are quite safe here, Simon. No one knows of my refuge. I come here to get away from them and I come here alone."

"Well, the first thing is—thanks Toni. I don't know why you bothered."

"It is nothing. I do not care for Colonel Jason. I do not like being called a wretched, gutless wop."

"No, I don't suppose so. But you took a bit of a chance, didn't you?"

He smiled. "Not so much," he said. "I had to be over on the yacht anyway on a task from Mantovelli. I had a good idea where you were. The rest was easy."

"But when they find out I've gone, they will know you were the only outside person on board."

"Not quite, my dear Simon. There are boys who make a practice of robbing yachts. They move like wraiths and swim like sharks. They know every boat in the *rade*. I have good friends amongst them. There is one concealed in the bows of *La Paloma*. When the alarm is raised he will make a great noise and dive overboard."

"I see."

"And", he went on, "their communication with the shore is temporarily cut. That same boy stole the plugs in the motor-boat."

"You think of everything, Toni. Did you persuade Jason to give me that half-hour of grace too?"

"No, I did not. It is what I wanted to talk to you about, Simon. He is a little mad, that one. Not much, but a little. He had plans for you. It is still rankling with him what happened on the road in the mountains, especially as the girl was there."

"Yes, but——"

He held up his hand and went on. "There is an inn, the *Auberge des Ciels Bleus*, on the northern face of Mont Ventoux, high up, not far from the summit. It is a ski-ing inn, really, and it is supposed to be shut in the summer. It belongs to Jason; it was given him as a present by Manto-velli for some task well performed. In fact it is never closed. There is a staff of Jason's servants in residence all the year round. There he entertains his chosen guests and does as he wishes. Strange things happen there. I have seen some of them. He hoped you would talk through fear and without physical injury."

"I damn near did."

"Then he intended to bring you to Mont Ventoux. He would keep you a prisoner until he could get the girl. Once she was there he would show her how much the better man he was than you—with pistols, I think, in single combat. He is a little mad, as I say, that one."

"How do you know all this, Toni?"

"Manuelo, the other driver, was waiting on the quay. He said he was detailed for Mont Ventoux. The rest Le Colonel told me himself on the yacht."

"What?"

"Yes. I had to speak to him in his cabin. He hates me, Le Colonel, and more so since that day on the road," Toni smiled a little at the recollection. "He hates me, too, because he cannot drive a car at all well and he is too proud to learn, and I know it, and I take care to show him up when I can. He is better with horses, they tell me. He wanted me to know what was going to happen to you. He had to tell me so that I, too, should know that his humiliation would be wiped out."

"But all this, Toni—you still took an awful risk letting me out."

The little Italian looked away from me. "Mantovelli's life is hanging by a thread," he said.

"He told me that, too."

"He likes the phrase. He is proud of it in some queer

168

way, I think. He uses it constantly, especially to his doctors. But if that thread should snap, and at any moment it may, I believe Jason intends to move in."

"To take over the empire? But could he?"

"Perhaps. He is the strong-arm man, the *chef de police*. He knows more of the secrets of the organization, more of the things they don't want uncovered, than anyone else. Already Mantovelli's grasp is loosening. He is eighty-three. It is a great age. He cannot hold things together as he did. Even now Jason is gaining in strength and influence. Money and power are the things he worships, and pride is his flagstaff. You will not live long, Simon, if he succeeds to the throne."

Silence fell between us as he finished speaking. I had been watching him and an inkling of what was, perhaps, the real reason for his rescuing me had come to my mind.

"You want him out of the way, don't you, Toni," I said. "You wouldn't be thinking of using me as a mobile gun-turret, would you?"

Again he gave me an oblique answer. "I like the old man," he said, his voice suddenly harsh. "He picked me up from the gutter or somewhere near it. That is where I was when I gave up driving and could not get a job. He has been kind to me. Whatever I have now I owe it to him. I don't want to see him at the mercy of that—that Hun. If you can beat him over this formula thing he must be discredited. Already he has lost face. Mantovelli offered you a job, didn't he?"

"Yes. How on earth do you know these things?"

"As everywhere else there are palace intrigues and whisperings. The pistoleer overheard the conversation. He is from Castelammare. He told me."

"What is the formula?"

"I do not know. None of us know, except Mantovelli and perhaps Jason. Something to do with horses, I think."

Like the wards of a lock falling into place several apparently unrelated remarks and pieces of information suddenly dropped together in my brain. "That might be it, all right," I said. "I must say, Toni, from what you have told me I don't much care for the thought of Jason about the place with Mantovelli's millions at his finger-tips."

He leant forward towards me. "We know everything about you, Simon," he said. "It is all there in black and white in Mantovelli's files. Every race you ever drove is there, so is all that is public about your war record. It is that, the war record, which makes Mantovelli think you are dangerous. And Mantovelli makes few mistakes about men."

"The war is a long time ago," I said.

"Steel doesn't soften or break, it only bends," he answered.

"What you really want, Toni," I said, "is for me to kill Jason for you, isn't it?"

At first he did not answer. "You must make up your own mind," he said then after a pause. "But I have told you how things lie."

Unnoticed by us both the orchestra had returned. I stood up and pushed back my chair. The opening bars of the second act thundered out. "Well, whatever happens, thanks again, Toni," I said. "I didn't fancy that second session with Beppo, much." I went out into the corridor and shut the door behind me. The great notes of the music stormed through the auditorium and, like muted thunder, reached me through the walls of the box. "*Le Crépuscule des Dieux*," I said to myself, and let the words hang there as I walked quickly down the stairs and into the street. As I got into the Bentley I remembered that there were other, rather more personal, questions waiting to be solved back at the cottage.

I left the car in the garage below the terrace and walked up the sloping path. All was in darkness. I stood for a moment, irresolute, wondering what had happened. And then I heard a faint splashing from the pool beyond the house.

The moon was sailing high in the sky, lighting up the whole countryside and touching everything with silver. I walked quietly round the corner of the house, past the flower beds and the cactus, to the edge of the pool.

A head came above the water, and began to move away from me. Its owner was turning lazily as if enjoying the cool caress of the water on her body. I bent down and picked up a pebble. With a flick of my finger I sent it spinning into the pool beside her.

It landed with a little splash. She threw up her head and looked around. "Simon!" she exclaimed. She began to tread water vigorously.

"Hallo, Sue," I said. "Well met, I think."

"Go away, Simon. I've nothing on!"

"So I notice. You seem to make a habit of it when we meet."

She turned and began to churn up the surface with her feet. I caught a flash of golden skin. "Don't bother doing that," I said. "The water is gin clear. Besides, you look very nice—even nicer than I thought," I added.

She laughed, swallowed some water and coughed. "Go away, you swine," she said.

Le Crépuscule des Dieux

"All right," I said abruptly. "When you've finished playing *naturiste* come back to the cottage. I want to talk to you."

I drew the curtains and switched on the lights. Her presence was there already. There were gladioli arranged in a porcelain vase she had found somewhere; drinks and glasses were on the table. The little room looked snug and charming and secure. I mixed myself a brandy and Perrier, stretched myself out in an easy chair and put the glass on the floor beside me.

After a few minutes the door opened and she came in. She was wearing flat-heeled slippers and a rough, towelling beachrobe of mine which she must have found somewhere, and very little else as far as I could see. It appeared to me to become her. But then it also seemed to me that almost everything did. Perhaps I was prejudiced.

"You're a beast," she said.

"That's about the least of the things I've been called in my time. Have a cigarette and forget it. You did look very nice, you know."

She sat down in the chair opposite to me, began to cross her legs and then, remembering the robe, changed her mind. Suddenly she started to laugh. "I was tired and lonely and I thought a bathe would do me good," she said. "I couldn't find anything to wear and, let's face it, I've always wanted to bathe with nothing on to see what it is like. I never seemed to get round to it, somehow. This looked a wonderful opportunity. You came back about ten minutes too soon."

I stretched out my hand with my cigarette case in it.

"What is that?" she said sharply, her eyes on my wrist.

I looked down. There was a narrow angry, red weal across the flesh where the cords had cut into me.

"That," I said slowly, "is where your boy-friend, Stuart Jason, had me bound up an hour or so ago. He threw me downstairs in London yesterday. That makes him one up on me. I don't quite know when we are going to play the equaliser." I looked at her steadily. "Are you in love with him?"

Her fingers trembled a little as she took the cigarette. "No, Simon, I'm not," she said.

"That isn't what they say in London. I was told that you wanted him but the General stopped it."

"That's not true," she said fiercely. "You know yourself the things people say. Goodness, Simon, the stories I've heard about you. If you'll listen I'll try to explain." She drew a deep breath and pulled on her cigarette. "Stuart took me out in London last year," she began. "At first I was dazzled by, oh, I don't know, the glamour, I suppose that goes with him or anyone like him with his history of success and then failure in a romantic sort of way. I was flattered, too, at his noticing me. I had never thought a great deal of myself, you know. Roddy was always the success of the family. And Stuart was so arrogant with other people and yet pleasant and charming to me. Goodness, Simon, it's so hard to explain—but he knew his way around rather like you do and when you have been used to fumbling boys——"

"Go on," I said quietly.

"Then I began to find him out. I saw that he was cruel and vain and that only one person existed for him and that was himself. I discovered that he was almost insanely ambitious and it frightened me. Yet, even then, though I told myself that I hated him, there was some horrible attraction about him, too. In Arles, in that ghastly hotel, I was terrified. I was frightened out of my wits about what he would do if he caught up with me. And then, when he did, he wasn't fierce or brutal at all. He was kind and charming; and at the château he was, too. I knew he was evil; I know now he is evil but—oh, Simon, that night in Arles, if you had only stayed. . . ." Suddenly she put her head in her hands and burst into tears.

"Are you in love with him?" I said harshly.

"No, no, Simon, I'm not, I swear I'm not. But don't you see, he keeps telling me that he wants me, that he needs me and loves me. When someone like Stuart tells you that it does make a difference——"

"Does it?" I said. "Does it, Sue?"

She lifted her head and we stared at each other across the little table. I didn't have to say the words. I stretched my hand out to her and she came into the crook of my arm as if she had been there always. Her lips on mine were soft and fresh. The robe fell open and I felt the silken sheen of her skin under my hand. Almost desperately I drew her to me. She was all I had to hang on to in the world.

There was a thunderous knock on the door. It stopped and was repeated. I sat up with a jerk, the present and its perils rushing back upon me.

"Quick—where is the gun?" I said.

Crossing quietly to the dresser she opened a drawer, took it out and handed it to me. I snapped off the light and went to the door. Holding the gun down by my side I thumbed back the hammer.

"Who is it?" I said.

"It's me. Roddy Marston. Open up," came the cheerful reply.

I freed the catch and put on the lights. "Where the hell have you been?" I said, as he walked into the room.

Le Crépuscule des Dieux

"I've come all the way from Toulon in a bus and I badly want a drink."

I mixed him a stiff one. I could cheerfully have put arsenic in it. He had a talent for making unwanted entrances. "You'll need this," I said as I handed it to him. "Legarde isn't in business any more." And then, very briefly, I told him what had happened.

CHAPTER 13

Ruse de Guerre

The next morning Roddy left early. He had got himself up in a striped singlet, a pair of linen trousers, dark glasses and one of those white linen deerstalkers affected by some Frenchmen on the Riviera. And despite it all he still looked as if he was in the parade ring at Cheltenham about to go out for the Foxhunter's Chase. There is something about these horsey chaps you can't disguise.

"Very fetching," I said as I poured myself some coffee and spread jam on a *croissant*. "I suppose you think you're the modern version of the man who broke the bank at Monte Carlo. You've certainly got an independent air. Whose racing colours are you wearing?"

"Legarde's—I hope. I'm going to find him, Simon."

"What good will that do you? He's been bought off."

"Legarde would double-cross his grandmother. If I can get hold of him he'll come back into the market pretty damn quick."

"Where do you think he is? I don't suppose he is back at Mont Boron reading those interesting books of his."

"He bets like a drunken sailor. He'll be somewhere playing the tables."

"Well, keep out of the fashionable pubs and off the fashionable streets and if you must open your mouth talk broad Yorkshire. They'll be looking for you, remember. Where are you going to start?"

Ruse de Guerre

"There is a black market currency merchant in Nice. Someone gave me his address when I came here first. He seems to know everything and everyone. I thought I'd try him."

"If he knows where I can find Jason without his bodyguard, I'd be glad of that information, too."

"I'll bear it in mind." He went off, whistling.

We spent an enchanted day, in the hills. On the slight chance that someone might have discovered our refuge in the cottage we had left it and taken a hamper with us and there, in a little lost and lonely valley with the whole coast below us and above us the sky hard with heat and burnished like a gun-barrel, we had let the hours go past, talking and making love and enjoying each other. It was a day filched from the ordinary run of life, a day which I hoped and believed was the beginning for me of something that would give some meaning to the years ahead.

When the sun went slanting down behind the hills and the cool of the evening came creeping up on us we packed up and came back to the cottage. Madame Huron cooked us a wonderful meal of *moules marinière* and veal done with a sauce of her own and served with tomatoes *provençales*.

We had our brandy on the terrace and as we were drinking it Roddy returned. He had located Legarde or he thought he had. The American was said to be staying in Beaulieu but he was elusive, apparently, and difficult to contact and the hotel had been evasive about his movements.

There was no point in taking risks and that night Roddy and I took turn about in sitting up with the revolver close to our hands. But nothing happened. It looked as if, for the moment anyway, we were safe.

In the morning, after breakfast, we sat under the

umbrellas by the pool, discussing what would be our next move. Beside me Roddy was busy at a table on which were cans of stout and two bottles of champagne. A large delph jug was also on the table and in this he was expertly mixing the stout and the wine.

"It's a bit early for that, isn't it?" I said.

"It's never too early for morning magic," was his cheerful reply as he handed me a tall glass. The stout, faintly touched with a golden bloom, frothed and bubbled. He filled his own tumbler and held it to the light. "This is a wonderful country," he said. "The stout is the price of champagne and the champagne is the price of stout."

I took a sip from the glass in front of me. He knew how to mix it, all right. And he was right, too, when he said that there was no drink to touch it in the morning. I looked at Sue, lazing opposite to me, cool and fresh in a white dress. I told myself that I was happy, that I had found peace at last.

"Well, I must get off," Roddy was saying, putting down his glass. "I'm bound to get hold of Legarde somehow, now that I've located his base."

"I think I'd better come with you," I said. "I'm not a bit happy about your barging around Nice dressed like an advertisement for men's beachwear. And, by the way, you have damn well got to tell me now. What is this ruddy formula?"

He laughed. Putting down his glass he looked mischievously at his sister. "After all, he's practically in the family, isn't he, Sue?" he said. "Very well, then. It's——"

An exclamation from Sue made us all sit up. She had turned in her chair and was looking down the terrace. 'What on earth is the postman doing here?" she said.

He was walking towards us, his canvas bag slung over

his shoulder, a letter in his hand. With a sense of misgiving forming inside me I got up and went to meet him.

"M'sieu Herald?" he said as I approached.

"Yes," I answered. "I am M'sieu Herald."

We talked about the weather for a moment or two and the prospects of the grape harvest. Then he handed me the letter, turned and walked off.

The address was typewritten and the envelope bore a French stamp. I put my finger under the flap and tore it open. The letter was brief and was also typewritten. The message it contained drove everything else from my mind.

Dear Simon,

Could you come over here as soon as you can? Mildred is up to something which I am afraid you won't like a bit. It has to do with her divorce. I can't put it all down on paper but I think you ought to know what is going on. I'm up to my eyes with this bloody house. I'll be on the site.

At the bottom was Maurice's scrawled signature.

My thoughts immediately leapt to Sue. Mildred had heard about us and was going to do something which would hurt Sue. That was my initial reaction. And it must be something pretty murky or Maurice would not have written so urgently. I looked at the letter again. There was no date which was typical of Maurice as was the fact that he had obviously got someone in the hotel to type it for I knew his dislike of putting pen to paper. Again, however, it must be urgent or he would not have written at all.

I walked back to the pool.

"What is it?" Sue said immediately, seeing the expression on my face.

"It's Maurice," I replied. "He wants me to go over there

right away." I couldn't tell them what it was about and I couldn't think of a good lie, so I left it out altogether. "I don't know what the old thing is panicking about," I said. "But he is panicking so I'd better get started. I'll be back as soon as I can."

As I drove to St. Tropez the ways and means which Mildred might find to hurt Sue went racing one after another through my mind. Mildred, I knew or thought I knew, wanted no more of me, but I also had a pretty fair idea that Mildred, as is the way with some women, did not want anyone else to have me. Besides, I had not been one of Mildred's victories. I had not come crawling to her to take me back, nor had I gone off with my tail between my legs, beaten and humiliated. In fact I might rank as one of her defeats, and Mildred liked to win. She would therefore spare no effort to harm Sue, of that I was sure. Well, she wasn't going to do it, or at least she wasn't going to get away with it unscathed while I was still about to stop her. Mildred had done enough towards playing havoc with my life. My thoughts threatened to get out of hand so I dragged them away from these matters and forced them to concentrate on driving.

St. Tropez was crowded. I was reduced to a walking pace through the town. It was mid-morning and the queers were beginning to emerge and make their way to the port to sit in the cafés and sip and sneer and titillate. Painted, indeterminate faces leered and peered at me from all sides. Bottoms waggled in tight trousers; strange shaggy heads swayed on scrawny necks. I was brought almost to a standstill by three of them tittupping arm in arm in front of me down the street. These creatures were dressed in identical cerise shirts with plunging necklines and they turned now and then to gibber at me. Another of them pushed his grotesque features through the open window and made a suggestion which I did not understand.

It was a relief to be out into the clean sunlight again. I took the narrow winding road that leads to the sea and turned off where the sign said *Parc de St. Tropez.*

The guard at the big entrance gate stopped me and scrutinized me. When I told him I had business at M. Kenway's villa he let me in and gave me directions for reaching it.

Maurice had certainly picked a delightful site. You came on it over a rise in the ground; in front of you was a gentle slope down to a tiny beach; two rocky, wooded promontories ran out from the foot of the slope and between these, about fifty yards back, Maurice was building his house. It would have a private harbour and was shut in and secluded on all sides. I made a mental note to make sure I was invited to stay once the work was completed.

The walls were up and the roof was beginning to go on. All about was the usual confusion which builders bring with them. Nearby a man was tending a cement mixer and I asked him if he knew where M. Kenway was. He looked at me blankly for a moment.

"But, M'sieu," he said. "I do not think that M. Kenway is here today."

"But he is expecting me," I said. "Perhaps he has gone into St. Tropez on a message?"

"Will M'sieu speak to the foreman? He is just there beyond." He pointed and I went over to a big, burly man with an unshaven face wearing a blue cloth cap.

"There is some mistake, M'sieu," he said in answer to my question. "But undoubtedly. M'sieu Kenway is away for some days. He told me he had business in London. He flew there yesterday."

Ruse de Guerre

"Are you sure?"

"But positive, M'sieu."

I stood for a second, rooted there, staring at the man like a fool, while the full realization of my crass stupidity flowed over me. Had for a mug by the oldest trick of all! It had, it is true, been cleverly mounted. Even down to the details everything had been just right from Maurice's dislike of writing letters or indeed of writing anything at all to the way I was sure to react to a possible move by Mildred against Sue. I thought I could see Mantovelli's fine Italian hand in all that. And of course he had in Jason someone who knew us, who mixed with us and the likes of us, was well acquainted with our friends, our wives and our failings. Under Mantovelli's questioning Jason would have been able to tell him all he needed—Maurice's rich man's hatred of writing, Mildred's proposed divorce; my ripening love for Sue, for Jason must know of that and hate me for it. Mantovelli would have put those three things together into a lure which he knew would entice me away from the cottage.

The cottage! Its whereabouts must be known to them, too. The address on the letter was proof enough of that. No doubt someone, Jason perhaps, had questioned Mildred and heard of it from her. They had got me away so that they would have the cottage at their mercy. And Sue was in it. The realization of what that meant hit me like a blow under the heart. For Jason, undoubtedly, would command the operation.

I turned on my heels and ran back to the car. Across the Esterels I drove like a madman, playing the *camions* at their own game, cutting-in in front of them, shouldering them aside and swearing back at the drivers as they cursed me.

Ruse de Guerre

So I came to the cottage, pulling up all standing with a judder of brakes below the terrace and running with all hell in my heart up the sloping path to the door.

It was open, swinging a little in the breeze. So were the french windows beside it. Someone had smashed one of them or been thrown through it. There was a great, jagged hole from top to bottom and broken glass was all over the flags.

Inside there was evidence of a battle. The table had been broken into pieces. One of its legs lay across the back of the overturned sofa. An armchair had been smashed into flatness on the floor, its back torn off and its arms collapsed. The dresser had been overturned and someone had kicked in its back. Books, flowers and ornaments were trodden into an indeterminate mess on the floor. There was a fair amount of blood about too. It must have been quite a fight.

"Sue!" I shouted. "Sue!"

No one answered. One of the curtains flapped lazily in the breeze. That was all.

Then I heard the moaning. It was a low sound of pain, cut off now and then as if someone were trying to control it. At first I could not tell where it came from. I went through the house but the other rooms were untouched and there was no one there.

Outside, I stood for a moment, listening. The sound came again. I walked round the corner of the house and there I found him.

It was Roddy Marston. He was lying in a heap in the flower bed, up against the wall by one of the windows. His right arm was doubled under him in a way I didn't like and his face was a mass of blood.

I bent over him. His eyes opened and he tried to say

something. He failed and a groan was again forced past his lips.

There was a wheeled lounging chair by the pool. I went across and brought it back to where he lay. Very carefully I moved him out from the wall and got him on to it. His right arm was broken above the elbow. There was no doubt about that. His shirt was in tatters, and when I stripped its remains off him I saw that his right side was a mass of bruises and broken skin. It looked as if someone had taken pains to kick in his ribs. I could guess who it was.

I pushed the chair into the cottage out of the sun and the glare. Then I got a basin from the kitchen and filled it with warm water. Taking a sponge from the bathroom, as gently as I could I cleaned the blood from his face. His nose was all over the place. He'd had it rough.

There was a bottle of Remy Martin in the kitchen press. I remembered putting it there the night before. I got this and poured half a tumblerful into a tooth mug. Lifting it to his lips I managed to force a good part of it down his throat. I wasn't at all sure it was the right treatment but I had to find out what had happened. He coughed and some of it came back. But what stayed down did the trick. A little colour came back to his cheeks and his eyes opened.

"God Almighty," he said. "That was quite something."

I put the glass to his lips again. He got it all down this time. He was tough all right. He put his good hand on the arm of the chair and tried to sit up.

"Take it easy," I said. "What goes on?"

"They bounced us, Simon. Only a few minutes after you had gone." He winced, and put his hand to his side. "This is worse than the fall I had at Wye two years ago," he said. "And I thought that was bad enough."

"That's where you steeplechasing swine have it lucky," I said. "You're used to being beaten up."

The brandy was beginning to take effect properly now. His eyes were open and intelligent and he knew what was going on. The chalky-yellow tinge which had been in his cheeks when I found him had gone altogether. He was also, I guessed, in considerable pain. "Give me some more of that," he said, pointing to the bottle.

I poured out another four fingers and handed the tumbler to him. He made an attempt to grin at me. "You're not a bad chap, Simon," he said. "Not as bad as you try to be, anyway."

"You can skip the compliments," I said. "And get on to what happened. Where is Sue?"

"She has gone with them."

"Gone? What do you mean—gone? Did she go or was she taken?"

"Jason said he'd let that big fellow, Beppo, kill me if she didn't go. He was in a fair way to doing it anyway. So she went. I was wrong when I said I could take care of him. I couldn't. He's a shade over my weight, and he uses an iron bar."

"Where did they go?"

"I don't know. I passed out."

A wave of despair hit me. We were beaten, and solely through my stupidity. For they might be anywhere by now and we had no hope of tracing them. They had Manto-velli's money behind them and the whole world in front of them. They had a start of an hour or more and pursuit was impossible. And Jason had Sue. It was defeat, utter and absolute. Presumably they had got Roddy's envelope, too, and all that it contained although just at the moment, anyway, I didn't give a damn about that.

"Did they say nothing that would give you a line on where they were going?" I asked him.

"No."

"I suppose they got your precious formula or whatever it is, too?"

"Yes, it was sewn into the lining of my coat. They hadn't much trouble finding it. You might as well know what it is, Simon."

"I don't see that it makes a hell of a lot of difference now. They've got it and they've got Sue, and they've gone. Still, if you want to tell me——"

"Did you ever hear of Pierre Sandale——"

Even with my invincible ignorance of things concerning horses and horse-racing I recognized the name. "That's the chap who made such a killing in our big races before the war?"

"Yes. He won everything. Classics and big handicaps, every damn thing. And half of the races were won by horses that breeding experts said couldn't win them. He won distance races with horses bred for sprinting and sprints with horses which should have been stayers. At first no one could understand it. Then the rumour got around that he had a hormone treatment which would make a donkey into a Derby winner. It wasn't a drug; it was a sort of supersonic tonic. And since it wasn't a drug it was undetectable. You can imagine what a stir it all caused. But no one ever proved anything. The old boy had a stud-farm and a racing establishment in Normandy and it was pretty well guarded. He was a hermit himself and practically never went to see his horses run. I suppose it gave him enough satisfaction to read the results and to know that he was pretty well unbeatable when he wanted to be. I wasn't in circulation myself then but that is what I've been told. My arm is beginning to hurt like hell. Give me another slug of that stuff, will you?"

I handed him the glass and he drank.

"Well," he went on, putting down the glass. "No one ever really found out whether the story was true or not, whether Sandale had in fact discovered the miraculous treatment they said he had. Then the war came and of course racing on any scale stopped. After the war Sandale dropped out of racing. He was very old; he was in bad health, for he'd been beaten up by the Germans and then last year he died. No more was heard about the treatment. Racing people have short memories and Sandale and his hormones were forgotten.

"But a few days after his death I got a letter from his lawyer. Inside was a sealed envelope and inside that was a long letter from Sandale. Although I didn't know it, it seems that in the Normandy fighting my father liberated Sandale's stud-farm. My father's armoured cars came into the stud-farm just at the time the Huns were beating up old Sandale. Maybe they were after the formula, too. I don't know. My father was always a thruster and he went straight in. He shot the chaps who were actually working over Sandale and saved him and the farm. My father was killed shortly afterwards but Sandale didn't forget him. He left instructions that I was to be sent the formula after his death. Naturally enough he wouldn't share the secret with anyone during his lifetime. That is what it is."

Exhausted by talking and the pain he leant his head back on the cushions of the chair. I handed him the brandy again.

"I half guessed it might be something like that," I said. "Mantovelli wants it to fulfil his last ambition. That is to win the Derby, isn't it?"

"That's it. He wants to give it to his bloody two-year-olds and I was damned if I was going to see him do it."

"Why?"

"Because they are a useless bloody lot. Legarde, give him his due, races on the right lines. He'd use it to make good horses better, not to make screws win the classics. Anyway, Jason wanted it for next to nothing. They've got too much too easy that crew and what they don't get they think they can take."

"He's got it for nothing now," I said grimly. "And I'm damned if I can see how we are going to get it back. Why didn't one of you use the gun?"

"We couldn't get to it. It all happened so quickly."

"All right. I'm going for a doctor for you. Lay off the brandy for a bit. I'll get Madame Huron to come up and keep an eye on you. I won't be long."

As I pulled up in front of the Hurons' house it struck me that everything was very quiet. There was no sign of Huron working amongst his vines nor was there any sound of his wife at her household chores inside. The door was shut and that in itself was odd. I knocked and there was no answer. When I had knocked again and waited I went around to the back and looked in a window. What I saw made me throw open the door at a run. Inside their tiny kitchen Huron and Madame Huron were gagged and bound in their chairs.

As I freed them I made my apologies. They took it all with the dignity I would have expected. Indeed their thoughts were much less for themselves than for Roddy and Sue for they had heard the fight in the cottage.

"M. Marston is hurt," I said. "And I wonder if you would stay with him, Madame, while I fetch a doctor."

Ruse de Guerre

"And Mademoiselle?" she asked.

"They have taken her," I said simply.

"And you do not know where?"

"No." I raised my hands. "I am helpless."

She put her hand on my arm. "But I think maybe I have news for you, M'sieu," she said. "When we were being bound one of them, he is slight with a small moustache, I think he drove the car——"

"Toni Veletti!" I exclaimed. "Yes, Madame?"

"He whispered in my ear. 'Tell him,' he said, 'tell him we go to Mont Ventoux'."

"Jason's hideout!" I said. "So that is where they have taken her. A thousand thanks, Madame. You have given me new hope."

I knew a doctor in Cannes, Paul Velain, a man of about my own age. He had treated me at the cottage for *la grippe*, and had attended to the hangovers of some of my guests and to Mildred when she had wrenched her back water-ski-ing. He had dined with us on occasion, too, so he was something more than a casual medical attendant. Luckily he was in and when I had told him something of what had happened he agreed to come at once.

Whilst he was inside the cottage with Roddy I got out my maps. *L'Auberge des Ciels Bleus* was on the north face of the mountain, Toni had said. I had driven over Mont Ventoux some years back as one of the things to do in Provence and to see the view. On another occasion I had gone there for the hill-climb. What I knew of the terrain told me that it would be unwise to approach by the southern and more direct route where my car could be picked out for miles against the beds of shale surrounding the summit. I would have to circle the mountain, go to Malaucene and make my approach from there.

Ruse de Guerre

I was still bending over the maps when the doctor came out.

"I have forgotten just how you say it, Simon," he said, snapping his bag shut. "But he is as strong as one of his own *chevaux de course*. But, of course, I must have him brought to hospital and X-rayed." He looked at me steadily. "This is, I think, a police matter," he said.

"You must do what is right for yourself about that, Paul," I said.

"Very well. I have given him a sedative and set the arm. For the moment he will be all right until the ambulance comes."

I folded up the maps. "Will you wait in the car, Paul?" I said. "I have something to settle with those who did this. I want a word with him before I go. Will that be all right?"

"Perfectly. But, Simon, I do not advise any more cognac —even as a medicine."

"Well," I said, when I was once more inside the wrecked living-room. "I hear you'll live."

"So he tells me."

"They've gone to Mont Ventoux. Jason has a hideout there. I'm going after him."

"I'm afraid you'll have to go it alone. But that is how you'd want it, isn't it? Better bring the gun."

"I intend to. Where is it?"

"In that." He nodded towards the wrecked dresser.

I bent over and pulled the piece upright. The drawer was stuck but after banging it about a bit I got it open. I put my hand in and took out the gun. I checked that it was loaded and dropped it into my pocket.

The sedative was working. His eyes were closing and his breath was coming more regularly and deeply as I turned towards the door.

Ruse de Guerre

Madame Huron came in as I left. "I shall stay with him," she said. Then she took my hands in hers. "*Au revoir*, M'sieu," she said. "She is lovely, Mademoiselle. And she is good. You are lucky—at last. *Bonne chance*, M'sieu."

CHAPTER 14

Duello

It was five o'clock in the afternoon when I stopped the Bentley, dusty and travel-stained, under the plane trees in the little street at Malaucene. Beside me was a café. There were a couple of tables on the pavement and a door with a bead curtain leading into the house at the back. There was no one about and the tables were untenanted. I parted the bead curtain and found myself in a dark, narrow room with a bar running down the right-hand side. A door at the back opened and a tubby little man with a round red face and bright intelligent eyes came out. The dust of travel had got into my throat and I was desperately thirsty. I ordered a beer.

"Have you been on the mountain, M'sieu?" he asked me, as he put the bottle and glass on the counter in front of me.

No, I said, but I was going up. Did M'sieu know the *Auberge des Ciels Bleus*?

"I have never been there," he answered. "But they tell me of it. It is beautiful but it is indeed in the clouds. And in this season it is shut."

"I know," I said. "But I have heard of it for the ski-ing, and I would like to see it now that I am here."

He gave me a look filled with curiosity. No doubt the comings and goings at the inn had not escaped the locals. "One moment, M'sieu," he said. Going to the back of the shop he called, "Charles! Charles! Come here!"

"Yes, Papa." There was the sound of feet on a staircase and Charles came at a run through the door into the shop. He was a thin dark slip of a boy of about fourteen who had his father's bright intelligent eyes.

"M'sieu wishes to know how to reach the *Auberge des Ciels Bleus*," his father said to him.

"It is very high, M'sieu, and it is closed."

"I know but I want to see it and to know what it is like for the winter. I want to come there for the ski-ing."

"There is a path through the pines. I will try to show you."

We all went to the door of the shop. Above and over us towered the great bulk of the mountain. Cloud ringed its top. Even today in the blistering heat of inner Provence in mid-June it would be cold up there, I reckoned.

The boy pointed upwards to where the tree belt ended. "There, M'sieu," he said. "Just below the trees, there is the road to it."

I went to the car and got out the binoculars. Standing beside him, I put them to my eyes. I could see it quite clearly then, a road through the trees, running along the side of the mountain.

"And the inn?" I asked.

"It is about a kilometre beyond, on a little shelf. All France is below you. It is very beautiful."

I thanked them both and got into the car. As I turned to the left between the houses and started the ascent I could feel their eyes following me.

At first there were cultivated fields on either side. Then little valleys holding lush meadows and ripening corn ran back into the foothills. Presently I was on to the mountain proper with wild flowers growing thick and running riot on either side of the road, their lovely scent hanging on the air and coming in the windows of the car. Soon, as the road twisted upwards, those wonderful vistas began to open out and I found myself looking down into all the secret corners of Provence. All about me and below me the green of the mountains and the gold of the fields were heightened by the distance and the brilliant sun. Then I was into the forest of beeches and pines climbing steeply through the corners and the air was getting colder and sharper every minute.

Where a convenient outcrop of rock ran down to the road I stopped the car and took out the glasses. Climbing to the top I stood under the trees which lined it and pointed the glasses upwards. I was nearer than I thought. Only a few hundred feet above me the track ran into the woods.

There was no sign or pointer to show that at the end of the track was the *Auberge des Ciels Bleus*. That was to be expected. Jason would not seek advertisement nor chance callers, not that he was likely to get many up here in any case. Nor, so far as I could see, were there any guards or sentries. I supposed that, too, was to be expected. Here in these lonely heights Jason could well consider himself secure.

Back at the car I got out a jersey and put it on. Through gaps in the clouds below me, down unfathomable depths away I could see the sun still striking hot on the cornfields, but up here there was a cutting edge to the wind as it came sighing and whistling through the trees.

Then I began to look for a place to hide the car. Higher up, too near the place where the track to the inn began for true safety, I found one. On the outside of a corner a path or ramp led steeply downwards. It was narrow and there was nothing but sky on the far side but

Duello

it had to serve. Originally, I fancy, it must have led somewhere, but a fall of stones had blocked the way not much
more than a car's length below the road. Very gingerly, I
backed down into it. When I had done so the offside
wheels were only an inch or two from the abyss. The roof
was now below the level of the road and she was at least
concealed from the casual glance. In any event evening
was coming on and I did not intend to spend much time
about what I had to do. I took the Smith & Wesson out
of the glove compartment and checked once more to see
that it was loaded and that the chamber was free. Then I
started upwards.

I took to the trees above the roadway to the inn and
walked along parallel to it, keeping my eyes open. It was
easy going on the soft turf under the pines and in a surprisingly short time I saw brightness ahead indicating where
the road ended. The boy had exaggerated when he said that
the distance was a kilometre.

I went more carefully then and kept under cover as I
surveyed the ground.

The inn itself was a long low two-storeyed building.
From where I stood I could see two sides of it. Round
the ground floor ran a series of arches. Glass doorways,
opening to the ground, filled these arches. The house was
set into the hill and sheltered on all sides by the woods
which grew around it. On the northern side these woods
had been cut away to give a view. On a clear day it must
have been stupendous.

The red Ferrari was drawn up in front of the main
doorway. No one was about. Nothing moved except the
thin rustle of the wind through the trees.

Taking a deep breath I ran across the narrow space of
open ground which separated the woods from the house.

195

Duello

No one shot at me. My heart pounding, I leant against the wall beside the nearest of the arches. From where I stood I could see quite clearly into the room beyond the glass door. I could hear, too, for the door was ajar.

What I was looking into was obviously the main room of the inn. It was large and spacious and light flowed into it from the surrounding archways. There was a beamed ceiling, a floor of red tiles picked out in white and a huge brick fireplace. Across one corner was a bar. There was a big, polished oak table with books and magazines on it, some high-backed Jacobean-looking chairs and one or two leather armchairs.

Beside the table with an envelope in his hand stood Stuart Jason. Sue was sitting in an armchair facing him. She looked frightened, and as if she was trying not to show it. My heart went out to her.

"Now," Jason was saying, tapping the envelope against his fingers as he spoke. "You understand me when I say I always win. Here is the precious formula Mantovelli was prepared to go to such lengths to get. I have it. I also have you. You see, Sue, it is not much use trying to fight me, is it?"

"What are you going to do with that formula, Stuart?"

"Keep it, of course. Mantovelli's life is hanging by a thread. He'll be lucky if he lasts a month let alone until next year's Derby. No, it's mine now. So are you, Sue."

The last words were added softly. I felt for the gun and took it out.

A faint noise behind me made me turn my head. What I saw caused me to flatten myself back against the corner of the wall, out of sight.

A big black and yellow Rolls came whispering out of the trees and purred to a stop in front of the house. A man leapt from behind the wheel and sprang to open one of the back doors.

From the car, moving with care but scorning the driver's proffered arm, Mantovelli got down. The driver went back to his seat and the Rolls moved off, out of sight.

Slowly, with his stilted, wide-legged, old-man's gait, leaning on his gold-headed cane, Mantovelli came up the steps and into the room. He entered as one accustomed to command and he looked Jason steadily in the face as he approached. A few feet from the table he halted.

"You have exceeded your instructions, Colonel Jason," he said. "I told you to bring the formula to me and I told you not to touch the girl." The words and the tone were incisive enough but I fancied that the altitude, the exertion and the tension of the occasion were all getting at him. Something almost approaching a gasp left his lips as he finished and it was only will-power, I thought, which cut it off short. His face, too, was a bad colour; it had taken on a mottled tinge which I had not seen on it before. Although he was clearly trying not to, he was leaning heavily for support on the gold-headed stick.

"You have had your day, Mantovelli," Jason said brutally. "And you have made your biggest mistake coming here. I have the formula and I'm keeping it. You don't matter any more. You are too old; you have lost your grip. I'm taking over from now on." He lifted the envelope to show it clearly to Mantovelli and then, with a gesture of finality, put it into an inside pocket.

The enormity of Jason's words seemed to hit the millionaire like a blow. His old hands shook on the knob of his cane. He was struggling to obtain sufficient control to speak. By an enormous effort he succeeded. "It is possible you may be right," he said stonily. "I may no longer be here to thwart you in your folly. But I think you have forgotten something." His glance rested directly on Sue. "Simon Herald is still alive."

"Herald! I'll settle with him in my own time."

"Take care he doesn't settle with you."

"Herald is only a glorified mechanic."

"He held your own rank in the war, though I notice he no longer has the affectation to use it. Did you ever hear of *hubris*, Colonel Jason? I thought not. You appear, however, to be suffering from it."

"That is enough, old man."

"Insolence!" He tried to raise the stick but the effort was too great. Suddenly his whole face suffused. A tremor passed through his body. "Why—" he started to say. "Why—" He staggered backwards, groping for one of the high-backed chairs. He found it and fell heavily on to its seat. The cane dropped from his fingers and rolled away. A spasm gripped him as he gasped for breath. He raised his head and looked for a moment full at Jason. His lips appeared to try to shape some words. Then he swayed on the seat and fell forward to the floor. The fingers of his outstretched hand just reached the cane.

Jason walked over and looked down at him. He bent over the body for a second and then straightened.

"Dead!" he said. "Dead! The thread has snapped at last." He gave a great wild laugh. "There is nothing to stop me now. Nothing!" His laugh rang out again. Then he turned to the girl. "And you, my Sue, are coming with me on my journey. Come." He strode over to her.

It was time, I thought, for me to come in. I put my foot inside the glass door and began to draw it open. It came out smoothly and without any noise at all. And as it

198

did so I saw the reflection in the glass. It filled the whole pane, suddenly, like an image jumping on to a screen. It was huge and menacing. It was Beppo.

His mouth was open, his arm was raised to strike. In his hand was a short iron bar. It was a weapon which he appeared to favour.

I ducked and whirled. The bar missed me by the fraction of an inch. I felt the wind of it as it went by. Putting the gun against his great chest I pulled the trigger, double action, twice. The noise was no more than the cracking of a dry branch and it was drowned by the roar of the Ferrari starting up. A look of bewilderment crossed his face, his features went slack and he keeled over beside me like a felled forest tree.

The Ferrari went off with the rush of a car whose clutch is let in too fiercely and too fast. I prayed that he had stalled her, but he hadn't, she kept on going. I took a wild snap shot at the tyres and missed. Then I was pelting down the track after it.

Through the pines I caught a flash of red as he turned up towards the summit. I breasted the slope and got the hill behind me. Then I ran for the Bentley as I have never run before.

Jason could not drive a car, Veletti had told me. He had taken the Ferrari and it was likely to prove a handful on the mountain for it was no child's toy but a man-size motor-car. That was, for the moment, all I had to hang on to—the fact that he was not my equal on the road and that I should be able to catch him. That and the certainty inside me that this was the showdown.

I brought the Bentley up on to the road with a rush. There was only one way he could have gone and that was up and over the top. At least I had not to try and think out what way he would take as I went after him into the clouds.

They were racing across the side of the mountain, ragged grey veils blown by the wind. Sometimes they were torn aside and vistas of the great depths below leapt into view. As we went higher there was ice on the rocks and lumps of dirty, packed snow were here and there on ledges and in crannies.

On the summit itself, by the observatory, the wind came howling round the car, biting at me and making me shiver through the jersey. Then I was down the first steep drop of the descent, round the corner at the bottom and into the shale. With nothing but those cliffs of loose rubble on either side of you it is like driving through the mountains of the moon. The road feels as unstable as the ground on which it is built and about to slip into infinity. But at least you can see where you are going on the corners and take your own line without fear of meeting something coming up.

I held the big car on the limit all the way down. But when I left the shale and dived into the woods I still had not sighted him. Perhaps he drove better than either I or Veletti knew. That growing doubt ate at me as I fled through the trees. I was getting down fast and I could feel the loss of altitude in my ears. It was essential for me to pick him up now for in a minute or two a choice of ways would offer itself to him. He could turn to the right for St. Estève or hold straight on for Sault. If he made the fork before I picked him up he might well escape me.

Then, far below me again, I picked up the flash of red. He had beaten me to the fork but the colour of his car had betrayed him. He had carried straight on for Sault. But he was further from me than I liked.

Duello

Cursing to myself I drove on my luck. I had to. I used all the road on the corners whenever I wanted it. Luck looked after me and I got that big car off the mountain in a way that would have surprised those who think the modern Bentley a town carriage. Only a quarter of a mile divided us as he turned up the hill into Sault.

There I lost him for a moment. It was pure luck that I picked him up again as I left the market place. He was below me, heading back parallel to his tracks, making for the Gorges de la Nesque. I trod on the throttle and went after him.

Leaving Sault the road runs straight and open for a bit. We were two big distinctive cars travelling fast on a little-used highway. He only had to glance in his mirror to see me and to recognize the car. Whether he did it then or later, or whether he had already realized that he was pursued and was leading me on, I shall never know. I am inclined to think that he had known for some time that I was after him, and had decided to do battle on ground of his own choosing. Whatever I thought of him I knew that it wasn't in him to run away. Well, the Gorges de la Nesque would be no bad place to settle what had to be settled between us.

We were climbing now, hard going against the collar, up towards those gloomy and forbidding labyrinths. Over the top we went and then began to descend the perilous twisting road which leads along the cliffs and through the very heart of the Gorges. It is a road on which you might not meet another traveller for a week or a month.

The vast and sickening depths seemed to reach out for our wheels as they clawed for grip around the bends. The advantage was with him for he could choose where he would stand and fight. I had to keep close to him, to give him as little time to think as possible. I was almost on top of him, now, crowding him hard and I could see him fighting the Ferrari as the tail came round at him. Once or twice the whole car slid outwards and it was its own inherent stability rather than his skill which saved him. He was not used to it and he was not good at it and I thought that he would not stand much more of it.

Even so it came sooner than I expected. It was round a bend immediately beyond one of the tunnels. The Ferrari must have spun outwards and he had stopped her inches from the edge.

I slammed on the brakes and swung the wheel hard over. The Bentley slid and scrabbled and came up all standing with her nose into the tail of the big red car. The impact moved the Ferrari even nearer to the brink. I saw her rock and thought she was gone, but she settled back and stayed there, balanced on a hair.

I threw myself sideways and banged open the door catch. The door gave and I fell out on to the road. A bullet spanged on the windscreen to hasten my going. I rolled over and back into the shelter of the tunnel.

There for a moment I stood, my back against the wall, getting my breath. Water dropped from the walls about me. There were pools and rivulets in the roadway at my feet. No sound came from beyond the cars. He was waiting for me.

Well, he wasn't going to get me climbing over the cars and presenting him with a sitting target. I moved back through the tunnel, the steady drip of the water drowning my footsteps.

At the entrance I surveyed the position. The inner side of the road was a sheer cliff some thirty feet high. But on

Duello

the outer side the roof of the tunnel sloped downwards and there were irregularities in the face of the wall which looked as if they would give foot and handholds.

I crossed the road and looked up. It would mean a climb of about twenty feet to get to the top. From there, if I made it, I could work my way to the road behind the cars. Involuntarily I looked downwards into the great grey depths. That was where I would go if I slipped and the thought of it made my stomach turn over.

I put my back to the edge and reached upwards. My hands gripped the first holds which I had marked out and slowly, inch by inch, I began the climb.

Once a lump of rock broke away underneath my foot and I kicked into nothing. My hands saved me then. My foot got on to a second support which held firm. I went on, my face pressed against the tunnel wall, my hands searching for each new grip and testing those I found. I don't know how long it took me but the rest of the holds were good and at last I was over the top. I lay there for a bit, panting and wanting to retch. I didn't know how near I was to the edge and I was afraid to look. Bloody fine hero I was. And Lieutenant-Colonel Stuart Jason, D.S.O. and bar, who killed men for sport, was waiting for me on the road below.

It seemed hours but I suppose it was only a couple of minutes before I roused myself. I crawled in from where I had been lying and then got to my feet and went along until I was sure I had passed the place where Jason and the cars were. Here the cliff over the road was lower. Below me was an empty stretch of road; up to the left a corner separated me from Jason. I put my feet over the edge and slid down to the roadway. Then I took out the revolver.

The sick taste of fear was in my mouth. I was in a blue

funk. I had to go round that corner into the open and let him shoot at me. He had said that he was going to prove himself the better man in single combat. Here it was. This was what he wanted and what I had told myself that I wanted, too. Here in this grim and lonely gorge no one was going to interfere while we came to the ultimate decision. This was it all right. This was the pay-off. And I wanted to run away.

I fought to get control of myself. I knew I had to make myself go round that corner. This was more than the pay-off between him and me; this was the pay-off for all those years since I had run away from driving. If I failed now I was nothing. And I had only three rounds left in my gun.

I tried to remember all I had been taught about gun-fighting. Fire single action and take your time—those were the ultimate verities of it. It was possible that he had been too proud even to learn those.

I put my thumb over the hammer and brought it back. The sharp little click as it came was quite clear in those silent heights. Suddenly, with that click, confidence came back to me. I remembered what I had been and what I had done. I remembered what Mantovelli had said about me. I remembered that Sue was there waiting for me. I had no longer any doubts. I knew then that I was going in. I took a deep breath and walked forward.

Steady now, I said to myself. Don't rush it or you are a dead man. Don't lose your head and go blundering in. Take your time to come on aim. Take it easy and *take your time*.

At the entrance to the corner I paused for a second. Then I took three paces forward. I was at the apex of the corner. I was around it and we were facing each other with weapons in our hands and on equal terms.

The whole scene printed itself on my vision with the impact and clarity of a photograph. At the mouth of the tunnel the two cars were at right angles to each other, the Ferrari poised on the very edge of the road. Up to the left, out of the line of fire and a little distance away, Sue stood by the Bentley.

Jason was behind the open door of the Ferrari. It gave him a shield. Somehow I had not expected that of him. Perhaps he had decided that he had too much at stake now to take chances. Perhaps the lust to win had rotted him; perhaps he had always stacked the cards.

He cut loose at me immediately with the big Webley. He had a hand on the door to give himself a steady firing position. But he was too quick, he was rushing things. Something went through the leg of my trousers. That was wild shooting at that range.

Deliberately I brought my arm up and laid the sights on his chest. With the door in the way there wasn't all that much to aim at.

A second shot plucked at my sleeve. He was beginning to get on target. It was time I came into action. My finger caressed the trigger.

And then, before my astonished eyes, it happened. The Ferrari was, as I have said, poised on the very edge of the abyss. Now, unbalanced perhaps by his hand or his shooting, it began to slide backwards. Its open door caught Jason like the embrace of an outstretched arm and took him off his feet. For a second one wheel hung spinning in the empty air. The door swung to bringing Jason with it and he fell backwards into the seat. Man and car together went out of our view, off the road and into the depths.

I stepped to the edge. Far below me now I could see the car turning over lazily as it fell. Then it struck. So far

Duello

down was it that I did not hear the impact. But I saw the tongue of flame that leapt up to devour them both.

There, amongst other things, I thought, goes Roddy Marston's fortune.

I turned. She was coming down the road towards me.

"You didn't kill him," she said.

"No. In a way I think he killed himself."

I threw the gun into the Gorge and went up the road to meet her.

THE PERENNIAL LIBRARY MYSTERY SERIES

Delano Ames

CORPSE DIPLOMATIQUE   P 637, $2.84
"Sprightly and intelligent."
>—*New York Herald Tribune Book Review*

FOR OLD CRIME'S SAKE   P 629, $2.84

MURDER, MAESTRO, PLEASE   P 630, $2.84
"If there is a more engaging couple in modern fiction than Jane and
Dagobert Brown, we have not met them."   —*Scotsman*

SHE SHALL HAVE MURDER   P 638, $2.84
"Combines the merit of both the English and American schools in the
new mystery. It's as breezy as the best of the American ones, and has
the sophistication and wit of any top-notch Britisher."
>—*New York Herald Tribune Book Review*

E. C. Bentley

TRENT'S LAST CASE   P 440, $2.50
"One of the three best detective stories ever written."
>—*Agatha Christie*

TRENT'S OWN CASE   P 516, $2.25
"I won't waste time saying that the plot is sound and the detection
satisfying. Trent has not altered a scrap and reappears with all his old
humor and charm."   —*Dorothy L. Sayers*

Gavin Black

A DRAGON FOR CHRISTMAS   P 473, $1.95
"Potent excitement!"   —*New York Herald Tribune*

THE EYES AROUND ME   P 485, $1.95
"I stayed up until all hours last night reading *The Eyes Around Me,*
which is something I do not do very often, but I was so intrigued by the
ingeniousness of Mr. Black's plotting and the witty way in which he spins
his mystery. I can only say that I enjoyed the book enormously."
>—*F. van Wyck Mason*

YOU WANT TO DIE, JOHNNY?   P 472, $1.95
"Gavin Black doesn't just develop a pressure plot in suspense, he adds
uninfected wit, character, charm, and sharp knowledge of the Far East
to make rereading as keen as the first race-through."   —*Book Week*

THOU SHELL OF DEATH   P 428, $1.95
"It has all the virtues of culture, intelligence and sensibility that the most exacting connoisseur could ask of detective fiction."
—*The Times* [London] *Literary Supplement*

THE WIDOW'S CRUISE   P 399, $2.25
"A stirring suspense. . . . The thrilling tale leaves nothing to be desired."
—*Springfield Republican*

THE WORM OF DEATH   P 400, $2.25
"It [The Worm of Death] is one of Blake's very best—and his best is better than almost anyone's."   —Louis Untermeyer

John & Emery Bonett

A BANNER FOR PEGASUS   P 554, $2.40
"A gem! Beautifully plotted and set. . . . Not only is the murder adroit and deserved, and the detection competent, but the love story is charming."   —Jacques Barzun and Wendell Hertig Taylor

DEAD LION   P 563, $2.40
"A clever plot, authentic background and interesting characters highly recommended this one."   —*New Republic*

Christianna Brand

GREEN FOR DANGER   P 551, $2.50
"You have to reach for the greatest of Great Names (Christie, Carr, Queen . . .) to find Brand's rivals in the devious subtleties of the trade."
—Anthony Boucher

TOUR DE FORCE   P 572, $2.40
"Complete with traps for the over-ingenious, a double-reverse surprise ending and a key clue planted so fairly and obviously that you completely overlook it. If that's your idea of perfect entertainment, then seize at once upon *Tour de Force.*"   —Anthony Boucher, *The New York Times*

James Byrom

OR BE HE DEAD   P 585, $2.84
"A very original tale . . . Well written and steadily entertaining."
—Jacques Barzun & Wendell Hertig Taylor, *A Catalogue of Crime*

Henry Calvin

IT'S DIFFERENT ABROAD   P 640, $2.84

"What is remarkable and delightful, Mr. Calvin imparts a flavor of satire to what he renovates and compels us to take straight."

—Jacques Barzun

Marjorie Carleton

VANISHED   P 559, $2.40

"Exceptional . . . a minor triumph."

—Jacques Barzun and Wendell Hertig Taylor, *A Catalogue of Crime*

George Harmon Coxe

MURDER WITH PICTURES   P 527, $2.25

"[Coxe] has hit the bull's-eye with his first shot."

—*The New York Times*

Edmund Crispin

BURIED FOR PLEASURE   P 506, $2.50

"Absolute and unalloyed delight."

—Anthony Boucher, *The New York Times*

Lionel Davidson

THE MENORAH MEN   P 592, $2.84

"Of his fellow thriller writers, only John Le Carré shows the same instinct for the viscera."   —*Chicago Tribune*

NIGHT OF WENCESLAS   P 595, $2.84

"A most ingenious thriller, so enriched with style, wit, and a sense of serious comedy that it all but transcends its kind."

—*The New Yorker*

THE ROSE OF TIBET   P 593, $2.84

"I hadn't realized how much I missed the genuine Adventure story . . . until I read *The Rose of Tibet*."   —Graham Greene

D. M. Devine

MY BROTHER'S KILLER   P 558, $2.40

"A most enjoyable crime story which I enjoyed reading down to the last moment."   —Agatha Christie

THE DANGER WITHIN   P 448, $1.95
"Michael Gilbert has nicely combined some elements of the straight
detective story with plenty of action, suspense, and adventure, to pro-
duce a superior thriller."   —*Saturday Review*

FEAR TO TREAD   P 458, $1.95
"Merits serious consideration as a work of art."

—*The New York Times*

Joe Gores

HAMMETT   P 631, $2.84
"Joe Gores at his very best. Terse, powerful writing—with the master,
Dashiell Hammett, as the protagonist in a novel I think he would have
been proud to call his own."   —Robert Ludlum

C. W. Grafton

BEYOND A REASONABLE DOUBT   P 519, $1.95
"A very ingenious tale of murder . . . a brilliant and gripping narrative."
—Jacques Barzun and Wendell Hertig Taylor

THE RAT BEGAN TO GNAW THE ROPE   P 639, $2.84
"Fast, humorous story with flashes of brilliance."

—*The New Yorker*

Edward Grierson

THE SECOND MAN   P 528, $2.25
"One of the best trial-testimony books to have come along in quite a
while."   —*The New Yorker*

Bruce Hamilton

TOO MUCH OF WATER   P 635, $2.84
"A superb sea mystery. . . . The prose is excellent."
—Jacques Barzun and Wendell Hertig Taylor, *A Catalogue of Crime*

Cyril Hare

DEATH IS NO SPORTSMAN   P 555, $2.40
"You will be thrilled because it succeeds in placing an ingenious story
in a new and refreshing setting. . . . The identity of the murderer is really
a surprise."   —*Daily Mirror*

Cyril Hare (cont'd)

DEATH WALKS THE WOODS P 556, $2.40

"Here is a fine formal detective story, with a technically brilliant solution demanding the attention of all connoisseurs of construction."

—Anthony Boucher, *The New York Times Book Review*

AN ENGLISH MURDER P 455, $2.50

"By a long shot, the best crime story I have read for a long time. Everything is traditional, but originality does not suffer. The setting is perfect. Full marks to Mr. Hare." —*Irish Press*

SUICIDE EXCEPTED P 636, $2.84

"Adroit in its manipulation . . . and distinguished by a plot-twister which I'll wager Christie wishes she'd thought of."

—*The New York Times*

TENANT FOR DEATH P 570, $2.84

"The way in which an air of probability is combined both with clear, terse narrative and with a good deal of subtle suburban atmosphere, proves the extreme skill of the writer." —*The Spectator*

TRAGEDY AT LAW P 522, $2.25

"An extremely urbane and well-written detective story."

—*The New York Times*

UNTIMELY DEATH P 514, $2.25

"The English detective story at its quiet best, meticulously underplayed, rich in perceivings of the droll human animal and ready at the last with a neat surprise which has been there all the while had we but wits to see it." —*New York Herald Tribune Book Review*

THE WIND BLOWS DEATH P 589, $2.84

"A plot compounded of musical knowledge, a Dickens allusion, and a subtle point in law is related with delightfully unobtrusive wit, warmth, and style." —*The New York Times*

WITH A BARE BODKIN P 523, $2.25

"One of the best detective stories published for a long time."

—*The Spectator*

Robert Harling

THE ENORMOUS SHADOW P 545, $2.50

"In some ways the best spy story of the modern period. . . . The writing is terse and vivid . . . the ending full of action . . . altogether first-rate."

—Jacques Barzun and Wendell Hertig Taylor, *A Catalogue of Crime*

Matthew Head

THE CABINDA AFFAIR   P 541, $2.25
"An absorbing whodunit and a distinguished novel of atmosphere."
                    —Anthony Boucher, *The New York Times*

THE CONGO VENUS   P 597, $2.84
"Terrific. The dialogue is just plain wonderful."
                    —*The Boston Globe*

MURDER AT THE FLEA CLUB   P 542, $2.50
"The true delight is in Head's style, its limpid ease combined with humor
and an awesome precision of phrase."   —*San Francisco Chronicle*

M. V. Heberden

ENGAGED TO MURDER   P 533, $2.25
"Smooth plotting."   —*The New York Times*

James Hilton

WAS IT MURDER?   P 501, $1.95
"The story is well planned and well written."
                    —*The New York Times*

P. M. Hubbard

HIGH TIDE   P 571, $2.40
"A smooth elaboration of mounting horror and danger."
                    —*Library Journal*

Elspeth Huxley

THE AFRICAN POISON MURDERS   P 540, $2.25
"Obscure venom, manical mutilations, deadly bush fire, thrilling climax
compose major opus.... Top-flight."
                    —*Saturday Review of Literature*

MURDER ON SAFARI   P 587, $2.84
"Right now we'd call Mrs. Huxley a dangerous rival to Agatha Christie."   —*Books*

Francis Iles

BEFORE THE FACT P 517, $2.50
"Not many 'serious' novelists have produced character studies to compare with Iles's internally terrifying portrait of the murderer in *Before the Fact,* his masterpiece and a work truly deserving the appellation of unique and beyond price." —Howard Haycraft

MALICE AFORETHOUGHT P 532, $1.95
"It is a long time since I have read anything so good as *Malice Aforethought,* with its cynical humour, acute criminology, plausible detail and rapid movement. It makes you hug yourself with pleasure."
—H. C. Harwood, *Saturday Review*

Michael Innes

THE CASE OF THE JOURNEYING BOY P 632, $3.12
"I could see no faults in it. There is no one to compare with him."
—*Illustrated London News*

DEATH BY WATER P 574, $2.40
"The amount of ironic social criticism and deft characterization of scenes and people would serve another author for six books."
—Jacques Barzun and Wendell Hertig Taylor

HARE SITTING UP P 590, $2.84
"There is hardly anyone (in mysteries or mainstream) more exquisitely literate, allusive and Jamesian—and hardly anyone with a firmer sense of melodramatic plot or a more vigorous gift of storytelling."
—Anthony Boucher, *The New York Times*

THE LONG FAREWELL P 575, $2.40
"A model of the deft, classic detective story, told in the most wittily diverting prose." —*The New York Times*

THE MAN FROM THE SEA P 591, $2.84
"The pace is brisk, the adventures exciting and excitingly told, and above all he keeps to the very end the interesting ambiguity of the man from the sea." —*New Statesman*

THE SECRET VANGUARD P 584, $2.84
"Innes . . . has mastered the art of swift, exciting and well-organized narrative." —*The New York Times*

THE WEIGHT OF THE EVIDENCE P 633, $2.84
"First-class puzzle, deftly solved. University background interesting and amusing." —*Saturday Review of Literature*

Mary Kelly

THE SPOILT KILL P 565, $2.40
"Mary Kelly is a new Dorothy Sayers. . . . [An] exciting new novel."
—Evening News

Lange Lewis

THE BIRTHDAY MURDER P 518, $1.95
"Almost perfect in its playlike purity and delightful prose."
—Jacques Barzun and Wendell Hertig Taylor

Allan MacKinnon

HOUSE OF DARKNESS P 582, $2.84
"His best . . . a perfect compendium."
—Jacques Barzun & Wendell Hertig Taylor, A Catalogue of Crime

Arthur Maling

LUCKY DEVIL P 482, $1.95
"The plot unravels at a fast clip, the writing is breezy and Maling's
approach is as fresh as today's stockmarket quotes."
—Louisville Courier Journal

RIPOFF P 483, $1.95
"A swiftly paced story of today's big business is larded with intrigue as
a Ralph Nader-type investigates an insurance scandal and is soon on the
run from a hired gun and his brother. . . . Engrossing and credible."
—Booklist

SCHROEDER'S GAME P 484, $1.95
"As the title indicates, this Schroeder is up to something, and the un-
ravelling of his game is a diverting and sufficiently blood-soaked entertainment." *—The New Yorker*

Austin Ripley

MINUTE MYSTERIES P 387, $2.50
More than one hundred of the world's shortest detective stories. Only
one possible solution to each case!

Thomas Sterling

THE EVIL OF THE DAY P 529, $2.50
"Prose as witty and subtle as it is sharp and clear. . .characters unconven-
tionally conceived and richly bodied forth . . . . In short, a novel to be
treasured." *—Anthony Boucher, The New York Times*

Julian Symons

THE BELTING INHERITANCE P 468, $1.95
"A superb whodunit in the best tradition of the detective story."
—August Derleth, *Madison Capital Times*

BLAND BEGINNING P 469, $1.95
"Mr. Symons displays a deft storytelling skill, a quiet and literate wit, a nice feeling for character, and detectival ingenuity of a high order."
—Anthony Boucher, *The New York Times*

BOGUE'S FORTUNE P 481, $1.95
"There's a touch of the old sardonic humour, and more than a touch of style." —*The Spectator*

THE BROKEN PENNY P 480, $1.95
"The most exciting, astonishing and believable spy story to appear in years. —Anthony Boucher, *The New York Times Book Review*

THE COLOR OF MURDER P 461, $1.95
"A singularly unostentatious and memorably brilliant detective story."
—*New York Herald Tribune Book Review*

Dorothy Stockbridge Tillet
(John Stephen Strange)

THE MAN WHO KILLED FORTESCUE P 536, $2.25
"Better than average." —*Saturday Review of Literature*

Simon Troy

THE ROAD TO RHUINE P 583, $2.84
"Unusual and agreeably told." —*San Francisco Chronicle*

SWIFT TO ITS CLOSE P 546, $2.40
"A nicely literate British mystery . . . the atmosphere and the plot are exceptionally well wrought, the dialogue excellent." —*Best Sellers*

Henry Wade

THE DUKE OF YORK'S STEPS P 588, $2.84
"A classic of the golden age."
—Jacques Barzun & Wendell Hertig Taylor, *A Catalogue of Crime*

A DYING FALL P 543, $2.50
"One of those expert British suspense jobs . . . it crackles with undercurrents of blackmail, violent passion and murder. Topnotch in its class."
—*Time*

**If you enjoyed this book you'll want to know about
THE PERENNIAL LIBRARY MYSTERY SERIES**

Buy them at your local bookstore or use this coupon for ordering:

Qty	P number	Price
————	————	————
————	————	————
————	————	————
————	————	————
————	————	————
————	————	————
————	————	————
————	————	————
————	————	————
————	————	————
————	————	————
————	————	————
————	————	————
————	————	————
————	————	————
	postage and handling charge	$1.00
———— book(s) @ $0.25		————
	TOTAL	

**Prices contained in this coupon are Harper & Row invoice prices only.
They are subject to change without notice, and in no way reflect the prices at
which these books may be sold by other suppliers.**

**HARPER & ROW, Mail Order Dept. #PMS, 10 East 53rd St., New
York, N.Y. 10022.**

Please send me the books I have checked above. I am enclosing $————
which includes a postage and handling charge of $1.00 for the first book and
25¢ for each additional book. Send check or money order. No cash or
C.O.D.s please

Name————————————————————————————

Address————————————————————————————

City———————————— State———————— Zip————————

Please allow 4 weeks for delivery. USA only. This offer expires 10/31/84.
Please add applicable sales tax.